LP
F
GIL   Gillenwater, Sharon

07-2112

Home Sweet Texas

	DATE DUE		$28.95
DE 05 '07 MAY 0 7			
JA 03 '08			
JA 29 '08			
FE 13 '08			
JE 25 '08			
JY 2 8 '08			
OC 0 6 '08			
FEB 0 3 JAN 2 0			
2/3/09			
6/12/P			

HOME SWEET TEXAS

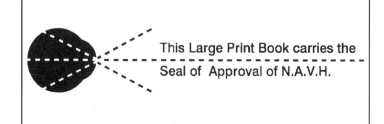

This Large Print Book carries the
Seal of Approval of N.A.V.H.

HOME SWEET TEXAS

SHARON GILLENWATER

THORNDIKE PRESS

An imprint of Thomson Gale, a part of The Thomson Corporation

Detroit • New York • San Francisco • New Haven, Conn. • Waterville, Maine • London

LIBRARY OF CONGRESS CATALOGING-IN-PUBLICATION DATA

Gillenwater, Sharon.
    Home sweet Texas / by Sharon Gillenwater.
        p. cm. — (Thorndike Press large print Christian fiction)
    ISBN-13: 978-0-7862-9958-4 (lg. print: alk. paper)
    ISBN-10: 0-7862-9958-4 (lg. print : alk. paper)
    1. Large type books I. Title.
PS3557.I3758H66 2007
813'.54—dc22   2007027435

Published in 2007 by arrangement with Harlequin Books S.A.

Printed in the United States of America on permanent paper
10 9 8 7 6 5 4 3 2 1

07-2112
Thorndike
Thom/Gale
11/07
28.95

For great is His love toward us, and the faithfulness of the Lord endures forever. Praise the Lord.

— *Psalms* 117:2

To Cade Michael Gillenwater,
our precious first grandchild.
May the Lord keep you as
the apple of His eye
and hide you in
the shadow of His wings.

CHAPTER ONE

Mesquite trees. Prickly pear cactus. A vast uninhabited land.

She was in the Southwest, somewhere between California and Texas. Maybe even Mexico. She didn't question how she knew it. General facts such as those seemed to come easily. Important things, such as why she was alone and on foot in the middle of nowhere, were nonexistent.

Turning in a slow circle, she searched the rangeland, silently praying for a glimpse of a house, a car, a power line — any sign of another human being.

Nothing.

The landscape was little different than what she had seen the previous morning when she had finally been able to climb out of the narrow canyon. Today it was a bit flatter, with fewer hills and long, flat-topped mesas. Rocky ravines cut through here and there, proof that it sometimes rained, despite the cloudless blue sky and dusty soil.

The grass was longer and greener than it had been the day before. Small green shrubs and the yellow-blossomed prickly pear added more color, as did a sprinkling of yellow and purple wildflowers and the scattered light green mesquites.

She had seen a light last night, way off on the horizon. It had still been there before dawn so it wasn't a star. Now, lining up on the arrow she had drawn in the dirt, she faced the west.

The light in the darkness, that tiny beacon of safety, had been miles away. Without any means to carry water, she dared not strike out toward it, across an unending and unforgiving land. She had to stay by the creek, though at this point it meandered more in a northwesterly direction. How far would she walk before it switched back around with one of those frustrating bends?

Still, she had water, for which she was eternally thankful. Water meant survival for a while. The small plums she'd found yesterday helped. Despite not being fully ripe, they were edible. She'd had five for dinner and six for breakfast as she watched the sunrise. The rest of the fruit on the shrub was too green to eat. If she stayed near the creek, she might find more of them.

Too bad fruit or water didn't help a pounding headache. Gingerly touching the knot on her forehead, she decided the swelling had gone down somewhat. The only good thing about a monster headache was that it kept her from noticing the mosquito bites so much. She checked her knee through the rip in her jeans. It was swollen, but there was no nasty redness around the big scrape. The cut on her arm had finally stopped trickling blood.

Was anyone looking for her? Would anyone even miss her?

Be strong. Don't give into fear. Hold on to Jesus.

"Lord, thank you for watching over me. For providing the water and the food. For keeping me safe from the animals last night." Coyotes? Wolves? She didn't know one howl and yip from another. Though they had seemed close, they hadn't come near enough for her to see them.

Even though I walk through the valley of the shadow of death, I will fear no evil, for you are with me . . . The psalm had brought her great comfort during the night, just as it did now. God was taking care of her; she was certain of it. But quoting scripture, recognizing plants and having some idea how to survive seemed so odd in light of the things she didn't know, the things she couldn't remember.

She took a deep, determined breath and headed northwest. Limping along through the grass and rocks above the creek, she prayed softly. "Lord, please send someone to help me. Someone who can tell me who I am."

Jake Trayner rested his hands on the saddle horn, the reins falling in relaxed loops along the mare's neck. He had followed a coyote's tracks for the past hour, not that he expected to come across the animal in the middle of the day. But it took him to a corner of his West Texas ranch that he hadn't checked in a few weeks.

He stopped at the barbed wire fence separating his land from the Rocking K Ranch. The flattened grass beneath the fence revealed where the coyote had wiggled through. The trail began again on the other side, then quickly disappeared in the rocks and brush. The ornery critter was probably watching him, tongue hanging out, a foxlike grin on his face.

"Fine. Go pester them for a while." Jake smiled as he thought of his best friend, Caleb Kincaid. He would be sure to mention that he'd given the coyote permission to visit. Get back a little at Caleb for teasing him about his piddly ten thousand acres compared to the Rocking K's hundred thousand.

He rode along the fence line, following it down the steep creek bank. The posts running up each side of the creek stood solidly in the ground, the barbed wire stretched tightly between them.

He dismounted in the shade and removed the canteen from Prancer's saddlebag. The horse sidled over a few steps to the edge of the yard-wide, lazy stream and began to drink. Jake took a long swig of cool water, then recapped the canteen and put it away.

Scanning the area, he listened to the chatter of sparrows and the sweet melody of a mockingbird. Thick green grass swathed both sides of the bank where the willows and mesquites protected it from the hot, late-May sunshine. The grass in the pasture wasn't as long, but it was still green and thick. The good rain from a week earlier was paying off. "Should move the cattle over here in a week or two."

Prancer looked at him, her plaintive gaze making Jake chuckle. Taking off his old battered straw hat, he wiped his forehead on the long sleeve of his blue chambray shirt. He squinted up through the lacy, pale green mesquite leaves at the noonday sun and settled the hat back on his head.

"Might as well stay in the shade a spell and have lunch. I don't have any pressing business."

He retrieved a brown lunch sack from the saddlebag before Prancer moseyed over to a patch of grass to graze, swishing her tail at a fly. Jake looked around for his dog, expecting him to appear the instant he heard the rustle of the paper. Licorice never missed an opportunity for a nibble. He whistled loudly. "Come on, Lic. Chow time."

Five minutes later, the dog came splashing down the creek and onto the sand beside it, water dripping from his face and feet. Jake supposed he was a bit odd looking, with the thick muscular body and legs of a Labrador retriever and the narrow nose and large, pointed, upright ears of a kelpie. His coat was predominately black, with a large white patch on his chest. The sprinkling of white on his chin and feet looked as if he had brushed against wet paint.

"I should have known you'd be playing in the water." Jake laughed as Licorice gave a hearty shake. The dog stared intently at him, backing up a few steps. He turned, looking expectantly over his shoulder at Jake and made a quiet, short huffing sound —

his way of asking someone to go with him. The dog tensed, poised to run. He rapidly huffed again, three times. Whatever he wanted, it had to be mighty important for him to ignore food.

"Hang on." Tossing a banana peel into the weeds, Jake hurried over to Prancer and slid the lunch sack into the saddlebag. He grabbed the reins, mounted and looked down at the dog. "Okay. Show me."

Licorice took off up the middle of the stream. Jake followed, guiding the horse at a fast walk through the grass in the dry portion of the creek bed. Dodging a weeping willow, he moved to the sand next to the water — and came across footprints of someone who had done the same thing.

He stopped the horse and dismounted, squatting down to inspect them. His father had taught him well, not simply to identify one animal print from another but to note the distinguishing features of a variety of tracks, from shoes to tires. During his years in law enforcement, especially with the Texas Rangers, he had expanded that knowledge. These were walking shoes, a size six or seven, the soles worn a bit more on the outside of each heel. The right indentation was consistently deeper than the left. The prints were undisturbed, not more than a few hours old.

He checked the creek bank, noting that the visitor had followed the cattle trail down to the water. He figured some youngster visiting the Rocking K had been thrown and the horse headed for home. The kid could have easily gotten lost and wandered over to Jake's land. In another hour, the whole section would probably be crawling with people looking for him.

Licorice was no longer in sight. Jake climbed back into the saddle and followed the tracks where they continued in the sand beside the water. He directed Prancer across the creek and up the bank to a trail worn in the grass from the cattle's habitual trek to drink. The trees and brush were sparse on that side, affording a good view of the stream, the footprints and south bank.

He knew to take nothing for granted, not even miles from the nearest road, and unfastened the strap on his holster. Approaching a bend in the stream, he put a little pressure on the reins, slowing Prancer. He moved around a cluster of mesquite trees and stopped.

On the opposite bank in the shade of a willow, Licorice sat beside a woman in the creek bed. The dog snuggled against her like a long-lost friend, and Jake felt some of his tension ease. Licorice was friendly, but he was also a good watchdog. If anyone else were around, he wouldn't have been so relaxed.

Jake studied the woman. Although he was less than thirty feet from her, she hadn't noticed him. And his dog was enjoying the attention too much to enlighten her.

She scratched Licorice behind one ear, her gaze never leaving him. Practically babbling, her voice was a little hoarse. "Such a good boy. You like that? Want me to scratch on the other side?" She moved to the other ear. "Does that feel good?"

Licorice tipped his head so she'd find just the right spot. Any other time, Jake would have grinned. Instead, he assessed her appearance. She was in rough shape.

The way her head was turned, he could only see one side of her face, but it was enough to know that under normal conditions, she was pretty. Her face, arms and hands were sunburned, scratched, bruised, dotted with mosquito bites and smudged with dirt. Her tangled, shoulder-length hair was blond, but it would take a good washing to reveal the exact shade. He estimated her height as five-three or -four; weight, one hundred twenty; age, the shy side of thirty.

Her light green tank top was streaked with

dirt and ripped in at least a dozen places. The tears, most of them small, could have come from barbed wire, mesquite thorns, cactus or a fall. Probably all of them. Several splotches of dried blood indicated some of the damage went beyond the material. She had wrapped a cloth strip around part of a long cut on her arm.

She was still talking. "How about under your collar? Want me to scratch there?" She paused, clearing her throat. "Doggie, you don't know how glad I am that you came back. What made you go running off?"

A rip in her filthy blue jeans revealed a badly skinned knee. An L-shaped tear on the other leg told him she'd probably caught the denim on a barbed wire fence when she climbed through it.

Jake refastened the strap on his holster to secure the gun and quietly eased from the saddle.

She looked at the license and rabies vaccination tags on Licorice's collar. "Are we close to your house? Can you take me home with you?" Her voice broke, and she threw her arms around Licorice's neck. Closing her eyes, she rested her chin on the top of his head. "I sure could use some help."

Licorice sympathized by licking her arm.

Leading Prancer, Jake half stepped, half

18

slid down the creek bank. Startled, she gasped and looked up, tightening her hold on the dog.

"His name is Licorice," he said quietly.

She gave Jake a wobbly smile. "It fits."

"Yeah, I thought so." A dark purple bruise crowned an egg-size knot on her forehead. "The first time I picked him up, I thought he was going to lick my face off."

Jake jumped over the water, walking slowly toward her. Tears etched a path through the dirt on her face. She made a valiant effort to wipe them away, causing an unexpected little lurch in his heart.

"He went to get you?" She tipped Licorice's face up toward hers, looking at him. "That's why you left me?"

The dog licked her chin.

"That's a yes," said Jake with a grin. "He can be real insistent when he wants something. Will lead me right to it. Though usually it's food, water or a toy." Not a damsel in distress.

Looping Prancer's reins around a willow branch, he took the canteen from the saddlebag and moved closer. Her focus dropped to his pistol, her light blue eyes widening.

"The gun is for protection, mostly from snakes." He didn't figure it would help her state of mind to mention the mountain lions, coyotes and bobcats that also roamed the ranch.

Jake squatted in front of her, careful to keep his distance and not make her feel too threatened. "Thirsty?"

She watched him warily and nodded. "I drank some water from the creek, but my hands make a lousy cup."

Opening the canteen, he handed it to her, noting that her hands trembled when she reached for it. He hated seeing the fear in her eyes. They were pretty, despite being red and irritated. Her lips were dry and cracked. He frowned slightly. She'd been out here at least a couple of days, not a few hours. Which made no sense. Even with Caleb and his sister, Megan, out of town, if anyone at the Rocking K had known about her, Jake would have been called to join a search party when they missed her.

Who was she? Why was she on his ranch? And what had happened to her? He caught himself before he slipped into interrogation mode and peppered her with questions. He'd get to those in a few minutes, after he made sure she wasn't badly injured. She probably needed food, too.

She tipped up the canteen, wincing as her lips touched it. The bandage on her arm was a green-and-yellow-striped scrunchie, one of those wide stretchy cloth things that women used to put up their hair. Knowing the name of it was an uncomfortable reminder that he spent too much time keeping company with the television.

Could she have been on his land the whole time? It was possible but not likely. Only two roads entered his property. He might not have seen her car go by the house, but he would have noticed the tire tracks. The other road cut through the pasture from Caleb's place. It was accessible only by a cantankerous wire gate that required a good dose of strength to open. Even on a good day, she couldn't have managed it.

She could have wandered in from the north side, but only on foot. There were no gates in the barbed wire fence that kept his cattle out of the cotton fields on the two neighboring farms.

"That's a nasty lump on your forehead. Looks like you took quite a fall."

"I don't know what I hit it on, but it knocked me out. I threw up a few times. I still get dizzy if I turn my head too quick. Sometimes even when I don't." She handed the canteen back to him. "Thank you."

"You're welcome." Jake glanced at her forehead again, guessing that she had a whopper of a headache. "You may have a concussion." He'd had a few over the years.

He pulled a clean white handkerchief from his back pocket, pouring some of the cold water onto cloth. "This should make your face feel better." He gave her the handkerchief and stood, easing the ache in his leg. "Any other injuries besides your head and the cuts and bruises?"

"I hurt all over, but nothing is specifically reporting in except for my head and knee. My knee is scraped, bruised and swollen, but it still works."

"You were limping. I can tell by your footprints. Lic led me this way, but it was easy to follow your tracks."

"I didn't think about that." She gingerly wiped her face, then fanned the cloth back and forth and folded it, leaving the least dirty spot on top. Holding it against her forehead, she closed her eyes. "You wouldn't happen to have some ibuprofen in that saddlebag, would you?"

"Sorry, no. Best I can do is a sandwich."

Her eyelids fluttered and she looked up, a gleam of anticipation in her eyes. Leaning back against the bank, she laid the handkerchief on the grass. "Manna from heaven."

Jake chuckled and retrieved the lunch sack from the saddlebag. "Roast beef from Taylor's Grocery."

When he handed the sandwich to her, she grabbed it, ripped open the plastic bag and took three bites before he sat down beside her. He touched her arm. "Easy. You'll make yourself sick if you eat too fast."

She nodded then flinched.

Licorice whimpered, nudging her thigh with his paw. She broke off a bite and gave it to him.

"Lic, mind your manners." Jake pulled a dog biscuit from the sack, tossing it to him. "You had plenty for breakfast."

She paused, eyeing the other half of the sandwich in the bag. "I'm eating your lunch." To Jake's amazement, she sounded apologetic.

"I'm fine. I already ate part of it." Just a banana, but he wasn't about to tell her that. He handed her an apple. "Nature's energy bar."

"Thanks." Laying the apple on her lap, she ate the rest of the sandwich.

Jake waited until she swallowed the last bite. Time to get some answers. "I'm Jake Trayner, owner of Fraser Creek Ranch."

"That's where I am? On your ranch?"

He nodded and smiled. "And I'm wondering why."

"I wish I could tell you." She wadded up

the plastic bag and stuffed it in the paper one. A deep frown wrinkled her forehead as she picked up the fruit. "The first thing I remember clearly is waking up sometime yesterday morning in the bottom of a narrow, deep canyon. It was too steep to climb up. But I vaguely remember stumbling around before that and being afraid because it was dark." She made a small motion with her hand, indicating her tattered-and-bruised appearance. "I think maybe I fell a couple of days ago. I was starving and super thirsty when I woke up yesterday."

"And even hungrier this morning."

Her frown faded, and she met his gaze, her expression softening. "I had wild plums for supper. There were about a dozen that were barely ripe enough to eat, but I saved some for breakfast, too."

"I'm surprised that any of them were edible. It usually takes another three to four weeks for them to ripen."

"They were so tart they made my eyes water, but I wasn't about to be picky." She looked away. "When I found the creek and later the plums, I knew God was looking out for me. That He wouldn't let me die out here." She paused, her expression bemused. "It's strange that I could be so certain," she murmured.

"Having faith isn't so strange." Unless you'd lost it, like he had. "Since you can't tell me why you're here, how about your name? I know all the neighbors. Maybe we can piece it together that way."

"I'm . . ." She hesitated, clenching the apple so tightly he half expected juice to squirt out of it. Her breathing grew shallow and quick.

Jake's intuition kicked into high gear. He spoke quietly but firmly. "Are you in some kind of trouble?"

"I don't think so. I don't know." Anxiety tinged her voice.

He gently rested his hand on her shoulder. "Tell me what you do remember."

"I can't." She looked at him, tears pooling in her eyes. "Jake, I don't remember anything, not even my name." Her voice broke. "I don't know who I am." Her hands went limp, and the apple fell in the dirt. She swayed, and Jake put his arm around her, drawing her against his chest.

"Easy, take slow, deep breaths." He paused, waiting for her to regain a bit of control. "That's it."

A shudder racked her. Then another. Jake wrapped her in his arms, offering comfort yet fighting the urge to protect her. A voice in the back of his mind yelled for him to keep his distance. To haul her to the sheriff's office and let him handle it.

But he knew he wouldn't.

"You're safe. I'll get you to the hospital. It's not big, but the doctors are good. They'll help you, and we'll figure this out." He held her for a while, murmuring a soothing word now and then, while his mind raced a mile a minute. Once during a car chase, he'd been hit by a kid in a pickup who wasn't paying attention. Jake spent a few days in the hospital with a concussion. He had no memory of the accident, the afternoon leading up to it or part of the day after. But all along he had known who he was.

She finally relaxed, and he eased his hold. "With a head wound like yours, it isn't unusual to forget what happened, or lose some time around the incident. What's the last thing you remember before waking up in the canyon?"

Breathing deeply, she straightened, and he released her. "Nothing."

Jake raised an eyebrow. "Nothing?"

"I recognized plants and trees and what was good to eat. I knew how to try to survive."

"Like following the creek so you'd have water."

"Yes. And that it might lead me near a house or where someone was working." She glanced at his hat, then her gaze skimmed the other side of the creek. "For some reason, I know those are mesquite trees, but I don't know what state I'm in."

"West Texas. We're about twenty miles southwest of Coyote Springs."

"It's not ringing any bells." She frowned, absently brushing at a muddy stain on her jeans.

"It's a typical small rural town, not particularly memorable."

Myriad emotions flickered across her face. Confusion, anger, but most of all, fear. Swallowing hard, she cleared her throat. Even then, her voice trembled slightly. "I don't know what I did three days ago, or any other day of my life. I have no memories of me." She looked up at him, and her voice dropped almost to a whisper. "Jake, I'm scared."

He whistled softly. This wasn't smack-your-head-and-forget-a-day-or-two amnesia. This was the full-blown stuff.

If she was telling the truth.

He narrowed his eyes, studying her troubled expression. Intuition told him she wasn't lying, but years of training and experience dictated caution and suspicion.

"When we get to the house, I'll call the sheriff, ask him if anyone has reported you missing. If they haven't, then we'll check the MPCH."

"What's that?"

"Missing Persons Clearinghouse at the Texas Department of Public Safety. If nothing turns up there, we can check for your fingerprints in the Texas driver's license database." She didn't have the slightest trace of a Texas accent, but with all the people moving to Texas from other states, that didn't mean much. Picking up the apple, he leaned toward the stream and washed it off. "Do you want to eat this now?"

"No, you go ahead. I don't think my stomach can handle anything else for a while."

He took a bite, thinking as he chewed and swallowed. "Then there's the FBI's National Crime Information Center —"

"You think I'm a criminal?" Her indignant frown made him smile.

"I seriously doubt it. They keep a missing persons' database, too."

"Oh."

He took another bite, then stood and held out his hand.

She took hold of his hand, muffling a groan as he helped her up. "You know a lot about this stuff."

"I used to be in law enforcement. Can you hang on good enough to ride behind me?" He took one last big bite and tossed what was left of the apple into the grass. The birds would appreciate the treat.

"I think so. I'll let you know if I start feeling wobbly."

"Good. I'll lift you up on that little ledge. It will be easier for you to get on the horse from there." When she nodded, he gripped her around the waist. She rested her hands on his shoulders as he lifted her a couple of feet off the ground, setting her carefully on the dirt outcrop.

He untied Prancer's reins and mounted, easing the horse over next to her. "Grab hold of my arm, put your foot on top of mine and swing your leg over her back." She followed his directions, sliding easily into place behind the saddle. "Now, put your arms around my waist, tight enough to feel secure."

She wrapped her arms around his midsection and rested the side of her face against his back. He heard a little sigh, but he wasn't sure whether it came from her or him. "That's good."

Better than good. He had the oddest feeling that he could get real used to having this woman nice and close.

It scared the bejabbers out of him.

CHAPTER TWO

Earlier that morning, she had decided she needed a nickname. Then she would at least have some sort of identity, even if it wasn't the right one. She'd chewed on it as she trudged across the range, something to focus on to keep the terror at bay. But she hadn't come up with anything she liked. Blondie was out. So were Spot and Scruffy — though given all her mosquito bites and bedraggled appearance, they were appropriate. Maybe Jake could help her think of something later when she wasn't so tired and her head didn't pound.

His suggestions probably wouldn't be all that complimentary. She resembled the Seven Dwarfs much more than Snow White. He, however, certainly qualified as Prince Charming. Or was that a different fairy tale? It didn't matter. He was a prince to her. He would have been even if he wasn't tall and muscular with short, dark brown hair lightly sprinkled with gray.

Waiting on the cement patio beside the screened back porch, she watched him tie the reins to an old hitching post in the yard. He glanced up, and she wondered if his blue cowboy shirt intensified the color of his eyes. *Or are they always the deep blue of the Pacific on a bright sunny morning?* She silently drew a quick breath. Had she been to the Pacific Ocean? She tried to search her memory, but it didn't take long to examine an empty space. Fear crawled over her skin.

"You're lookin' mighty thoughtful."

When she realized he had caught her staring, warmth stole into her cheeks. She hoped the sunburn hid it. "I've been trying to come up with a nickname for myself. Something better than one of Snow White's henchmen."

He smiled and turned on the faucet beside the house, using a hose to put more water in an old metal washtub for Prancer. Licorice immediately came over, and Jake held the end of the hose near the edge of the tub so the dog could lap water from it. "Don't like Sneezy or Sleepy?"

"Or Grumpy or Dopey." She watched them for a minute, smiling at their teamwork. "Do all dogs do that?"

"Not all. He's the first one I've had that does." His gaze ran over her. "How about Dusty?"

She smiled and leaned back against the door frame. "That's not one of the Seven Dwarfs. Even if it does fit."

He shrugged, giving her a lopsided grin.

Feeling entirely too susceptible to his charm, she looked away, studying the house instead of its owner. It was easy to distinguish the original two rooms and to see where various additions had been made over the years. The building had a sense of history, of being well used.

And lonely. She glanced around, wondering what prompted such a strong impression. A couple of new boards indicated recent repairs to the porch floor. Beyond the porch, half of the outside wall sparkled with a fresh coat of white paint, increasing the dinginess of the other half, yellowed from years of Texas heat.

Four empty Mexican ceramic pots sat under a pecan tree in the yard, their vivid colors long faded. How long had it been since flowers welcomed family and visitors? How long since the yard had echoed with the sound of children's laughter?

"You live here alone?"

Jake turned off the faucet and opened the

screen door to the porch. She followed him inside. "Most of the time, and it shows. Right now, my aunt Lynda is staying with me for a few months while she restores an old house in town." A ghost of a smile flitted across his face. "Come on in, Sunni."

"As in sunburn?"

He shook his head, his eyes darkening minutely. "As in your smile."

That was the nicest thing anyone had said to her in . . . oh, at least two days. Maybe ever. "You're sweet."

"Yeah, Licorice tells me that all the time." He opened the back door, motioning for her to go inside.

Cool air enveloped her as she stepped into the kitchen, prompting a relieved sigh. She walked over to the air conditioner humming away in the window and stood in front of it.

Licorice drank noisily from a water bowl in the corner, then sprawled on the cool wooden floor nearby, panting heavily. She rubbed the toe of her shoe lightly against his shoulder. "Poor dog, you about wore yourself out."

Jake hung his hat on a rack by the door. "He loves it, though he did run a little harder than normal coming home." Opening the refrigerator, he removed a half-gallon bottle of Gatorade. "I have iced tea, too, but this is better for now. It heads off dehydration faster and helps restore your electrolyte balance."

"Thanks." Suddenly feeling woozy, she pulled out a chair and abruptly sat down at the round oak table. "I need to restore my balance somehow."

"You okay?" He glanced over his shoulder as he opened a cabinet door, revealing neat rows of tall blue glasses.

"Dizzy and tired. My head is killing me." She laid her arm on the table, resting her cheek on it and closed her eyes. She heard him cross the room, set down two glasses, and pour the Gatorade.

"Here's some Tylenol. That will have to do until the doctor looks at you. When I had a concussion, they wouldn't let me take anything else for about four days. You can rest on the couch while I unsaddle Prancer and put her away."

"I'm too dirty," she mumbled, not bothering to open her eyes, not sure she could. She needed a bath, but it would be shame to drown after struggling so hard to survive.

"I'll throw a sheet over it, though it's nothing fancy."

No, it wouldn't be. He was solid and dependable, capable and kind. Not fancy. She wondered vaguely if she was foolish to trust him. Then wondered why she shouldn't trust someone who treated her with tender care. Not that she had a choice anyway.

She listened to the fading tap of his boots on the floor as he went down the hall. He returned a few minutes later, and she opened her eyes, watching him unfurl a blue sheet and spread it over the predominantly brown-and-rust Southwestern-style couch.

He added a pillow, then walked toward her. "Your bedroll is ready, ma'am."

She sat up with a tired smile, reaching for the glass and pills. "I would have paid you a fortune for a real bedroll last night." He waited for her to take a long drink and set down the glass, then held out his hand. When she took hold of it, he gently pulled her up to stand.

"But more for four-wheel drive?" He slipped his arm around her waist and guided her toward the sofa.

"Too rough. Needed some of Tinkerbell's fairy dust to fly out of there." Groaning, she eased down on the couch. "How can I remember Snow White and the Dwarfs and Tinkerbell and not even know my own name?"

"You got a thing for fairy tales?" Though his smile held a hint of teasing, kindness softened his eyes. He understood how frightened she was, how badly she needed to smile.

"Maybe. Is there a Dancer to go with Prancer?"

"Nope. Caz. It's short for Cazador." He watched her closely as she lay down. "I left him in the pasture by the barn, but he's probably in the corral by now."

"No Donner and Blitzen?"

"I let Cowboy Santa keep them. How do you think the cowboys get their Christmas presents?"

"That's a country song. I heard it last Christmas." An image of a car dashboard flashed through her mind, along with a few notes from the song. Gasping softly, she tried to mentally grab the thought and pull it into focus, but it vanished as quickly as it had come.

"Hey, you remembered something. Anything besides hearing the song?"

"A few notes of music and a flash of a dashboard, but nothing that tells me what kind of car it was. Maybe I was listening to the car radio?"

"Sounds reasonable." Jake sat down on the sturdy wooden coffee table, curling his hand around hers.

Security in a man's hand. She'd felt it

before, that everything would be all right because he was there. Jake instilled those feelings in her simply by his presence. But it seemed as if another man had, too. Was it possible to have a husband and not know it? She wasn't wearing a ring. Nor was there a faded line on her finger indicating she usually wore one. That didn't mean there wasn't someone special in her life. What an awful thought! To possibly be in love and not even remember it — or him.

Maybe Jake reminded her of her father. Surely, she'd had a father. Sudden tears stung her eyes.

"What's goin' on?" he asked quietly.

She blinked back the moisture. "A momentary pity-party."

He lightly brushed his thumb over her fingers. "You're entitled."

If she wasn't careful, she'd lose it. She reached deep, shoving the despair and fear aside. For now. She didn't know how long she could keep them from overwhelming her. "Nah. It's a waste of energy."

"I like your spunk."

"Is that what it is? Thought I was just stubborn."

"My daddy always said stubborn was just another word for determination. I think when the Lord passed that out, you got more than your share. Otherwise, you probably wouldn't be here." He released her hand and stood. "I'll call the sheriff and put Prancer away. Then we'll go to the emergency room."

"Take your time." *So tired.* "I'll just sleep." The pillowcase was soft and smooth against her skin. It smelled fresh, as if it had dried outdoors on a line. It would be a long time before she took a pillow for granted again.

"Do you trust the sheriff?" Jake made her feel safe. She didn't think anyone else could.

"Completely. I used to be his deputy. He was a good mentor, encouraged me to join the Highway Patrol, then the Texas Rangers."

No wonder she felt secure. An honest-to-goodness Texas Ranger. And a rancher? She supposed a man could do both. "So you're a Ranger now?"

A shadow passed over his countenance, and he looked away. "I quit two years ago. I'll be back in a few minutes." Turning abruptly, he hurried down the hall.

Licorice wedged himself between the coffee table and couch, lying down with a big sigh. She rested her hand on his back, burrowing her fingers into his black fur. He would watch over her. So would Jake. But for how long?

■ ■ ■ ■

Jake jiggled his leg, being careful to keep the heel of his boot off the tile floor of the hospital emergency waiting room. He'd already received a stern scowl from the old biddy across the lobby when he'd let his foot slip and tapped out a staccato beat for all of five seconds.

He couldn't help it. He hated hospitals, especially emergency rooms. He'd almost died in one. Key word being *almost.* For that reason alone, he was thankful for hospitals in general — as long as he didn't have to step inside one.

Maybe it wouldn't have been so bad if a car-wreck victim hadn't come in shortly after the nurse shooed him out of Sunni's curtained-off cubicle. The wailing siren, the doctor and nurses scrambling to meet the ambulance, and the medics calling out stats as they pushed the gurney through the wide doors and down the hall brought back too many memories.

Memories of pain, fear and sorrow so deep not even hovering death could over-shadow it. Even then, he would gladly have given his life for Deputy Pam Johnson's. But she had drawn her last shuddering breath a second before he collapsed beside her on the apartment floor.

That afternoon haunted his dreams, burdened his thoughts. Some people thought he was a coward. But the pleading in a little girl's eyes — not his own fear — had stilled his hand on the trigger. It had cost the life of a fine woman and put him in the hospital for weeks. He'd left the Rangers because he didn't know if he could cut it anymore, and he wasn't about to risk anyone else's life to find out. If that made him a coward, so be it.

His aunt touched his arm, the half-dozen thin copper bangles on her wrist jingling lightly. "Hon, why don't you go outside and get some fresh air. It'll be a while before they get to Sunni. I'll holler at you when I see the doctor heading our way."

Jake stopped moving his foot and took a deep breath, forcing himself to sit back in the uncomfortable green plastic chair and pretend to relax. "Sorry. Hospitals make me jittery."

"And for good reason." She picked up her purse. "How about getting me something to drink?"

"Sure. Want your usual root beer?" He stood, waving away her offer of money.

"And some chips or something. I didn't

have much lunch."

Jake's stomach rumbled as he walked around the corner to the vending machines. He bought a couple of packages of tortilla chips and two Hershey bars. Tucking the candy in his shirt pocket, he slid a dollar into the beverage machine and punched the button for the root beer. The can rattled down the chute, clanking as it hit the bottom.

He inserted another dollar and debated between a bottle of water and something with a little kick. The need for caffeine won out. He removed the root beer and punched the button for a Dr Pepper, cringing as its descent was even louder. No wonder the machines were tucked away behind a fake wall.

He wandered back toward the waiting room, casting a glance toward the closed double doors leading to the treatment area. Was Sunni afraid being in there by herself? Had the doctor even seen her before bedlam broke loose? Maybe he should go check on her.

His aunt was attempting a conversation with Ms. Grumpy. Typical. Lynda never met a stranger and almost always left having made a friend. Except for her ex-husband. That creep had broken her tender heart one too many times. After he'd had another fling, she'd finally divorced him five years earlier and moved back to Coyote Springs.

She looked good at fifty-seven. A little overweight, maybe, but not by more than ten or fifteen pounds. He assumed she had some gray hair, but he'd never seen it. Until she retired from her legal secretary job six months earlier, it had been a medium brown. Now it was short, red and kind of spiky. Made him think of a redheaded porcupine who wore big dangling earrings. But he'd never tell her that.

Jake sat down and handed her the soda and chips. He pulled a candy bar from his pocket, giving it to her with a smile. "Figured we could use a little extra nourishment."

Lynda laughed and laid it on the table beside her. "I don't know how nourishing it is, but I'll enjoy every bite." She glanced at the woman across from them, who now had her nose buried in a magazine. Lowering her voice, she leaned toward Jake. "The sheriff's car just pulled into the parking lot."

"He'll probably check on the wreck victim first." Jake stood and set his soda and food on the table next to his aunt's. "I'm going to see how Sunni's doing. Keep Toby out here until I get back."

Lynda's eyes sparkled. "Oh, I think I can accomplish that."

Smiling, Jake walked across the lobby. His aunt had a special fondness for Sheriff Toby Ratcliff. Given how the widowed sheriff's stern demeanor softened the instant he saw Lynda, Jake figured he had a special fondness for her, too. She'd changed since she'd retired and became half owner of the only women's clothing store in town. Her tailored business clothes had been replaced with colorful outfits and clunky jewelry. She was more relaxed and lighthearted than he'd ever seen her.

Jake pressed the call button by the locked entry into the emergency room treatment area and stood in front of the little camera, waiting to give his name and who he wanted to check on. The speaker clicked on. "Come on in, Jake."

There were some advantages to being well-known in a small town. He pushed through the double doors and walked down the hall.

Jake paused outside the closed curtain on Sunni's cubicle. He heard a doctor talking quietly and saw a nurse's legs beneath the curtain as she moved from one end of the bed to the other. He recognized the voice. Doc Hampton was Jake's doctor, too. Since another physician had been on duty when they came in, he figured Doc was called as backup when the E.R. got too busy.

The nurse pushed the curtain partially aside and stepped out from behind it. When she spotted Jake, she smiled and motioned for him to enter. "I was just going to get you."

"Thanks." Jake walked in, sidestepping out of her way. He nodded to the gray-haired doctor through the opening in the curtain, then peeked around it to look at Sunni. She'd changed into a hospital gown, but they hadn't cleaned up the cuts and scratches yet.

Relief spread across her face, prompting him to move closer. He would have taken hold of her hand, but it had a needle in it, the tube attached to an IV bag hanging above the bed. Half-a-dozen cords ran from beneath the hospital gown to the cardiac monitor. A blood-pressure cuff was wrapped around her arm, its cord also going to the monitor. Another cord from the same machine was attached to a clip on the end of her finger to measure her pulse and oxygen level.

Jake barely controlled a shudder. It was all frighteningly familiar. "How ya doin', sunshine?"

"Okay. It feels good to lie down." She smiled ruefully. "Even if the mattress is a little hard."

Doc Hampton reached across the bed to shake Jake's hand. "Her condition confirms that she'd been out there at least a couple days. Because she'd found water, she could have survived for a while longer." He looked at Sunni. "You're a tough young lady, but I'm glad you won't have to endure any more than you already have. I've ordered a CT scan of your brain to check for bleeding or injuries."

Sunni's eyes widened. Jake rested his hand on her shoulder and felt her relax.

"I doubt we'll find anything, but I'd be remiss if I didn't make certain. I want to keep you overnight for observation and make sure there are no hidden problems." The doctor motioned toward her arm. "Tend to those cuts and scrapes. Sunni —" He paused and glanced at Jake. "I'm glad you gave her that nickname. Sounds a whole lot better than Jane Doe."

"Fits better, too." Jake smiled down at her.

"For one thing I'm still alive." Sunni grimaced. "Isn't that what they call women in the morgue when they don't know their names?"

How did she know that? Jake studied her

innocent expression. Maybe it fell into the same category as recognizing mesquite trees. Or from watching television. "That's right."

"We use it in hospitals, too, when a patient is very much alive but we can't identify her," said the doctor. "Sunni, do you have any questions?"

She laughed softly, the sound whispering across Jake's heart like a soft summer breeze. "Dozens, all echoing around in the vast cavern of my mind. But the one worrying me most right now is how I'm going to pay for all this."

"I'll let the hospital administrator sort it out. I'm sure there are funds in some program or another to handle this kind of situation. You just concentrate on resting and healing up." Doc Hampton scribbled something on her chart and stuck the pen into the pocket of his white coat.

"A nurse will be here shortly to take you for the CT scan then get you settled in your room. In the meantime, Jake, I need you to fill in some blanks." He headed for the door.

"All right. I'll be there in a minute."

Sunni took a deep breath and met Jake's gaze. "Will you come by my room before you leave?"

"Sure. My aunt is waiting out in the lobby.

47

She wants to meet you, give you a little moral support."

She swallowed hard. "Thanks. I'll take all of that I can get."

"Don't worry. We aren't going to dump you here and leave you." Though a part of him wished he could. He'd lived alone for a long time. Solitude was comfortable. He liked his life just the way it was. His aunt and a few close friends were all he needed for companionship. In fact, he would be glad when his aunt moved into her own place again. As much as he loved her and had enjoyed having her visit for about a week, he missed having his house all to himself.

"I don't feel right imposing on you. You've already been so kind." She smoothed the tape holding the IV needle in place, then looked back up at him. "But I'm scared, Jake, and you make me feel safe."

A nurse came bustling into the room. "OK, my dear, let's go take your picture. Then we'll get you cleaned up and take care of those cuts and scrapes." She removed the blood-pressure cuff from Sunni's arm and the oxygen-sensor clip from her finger. Next, she unhooked all the other cords from the monitor and plugged them into a portable unit that she hung on the bed frame.

Grabbing a bag with Sunni's clothes, she plopped it near her feet.

Unlocking the wheels on the bed, she shoved it toward the door. "She'll be in Room 218. Give us about an hour to get her cleaned up and settled."

Jake followed her out of the room, catching up to walk briefly alongside Sunni. "I'll see you in a bit."

"Thanks."

He stopped at the nurses' station and watched them go down the hall. As the nurse maneuvered the bed around a corner, Sunni glanced back at him, giving him a wobbly smile.

Jake nodded but couldn't smile back, not when she'd chiseled a crack in the nice tidy walls he'd built to keep people at a distance.

Doc came out of a room nearby and motioned for Jake to join him. He closed the door to the small employee lounge, poured himself a cup of coffee and sprawled in a chair in the corner. Jake sat down across from him.

"Do you think Sunni is telling the truth about losing her memory?" Doc Hampton blew on the coffee to cool it.

"I haven't seen any indication that she's lying." Was he looking for it? Or was he so captivated by her that he ignored things he should have picked up on? Maybe two years away from the Rangers had made him rusty — and soft when it came to a certain blond, blue-eyed woman. "I met quite a few people with amnesia while I was in law enforcement. They usually said about the same thing — 'No, officer, I don't remember how I came to be driving that stolen car.' "

The doctor chuckled and took a sip of coffee. "I don't see much memory loss other than with my elderly patients who have dementia. I've run into it a few times with head injuries, but it's usually involved the time around the accident. Had one patient who remembered the past just fine, but lost his ability to retain new memories. Other things can cause it — a tumor, drugs, toxins. That's one reason I'm doing the CT scan and a passel of lab work."

Jake frowned and stretched his legs out in front of him. "You think she might have a brain tumor?"

"It's possible, but they aren't very common. If she snaps out of it in a day or two, I'll blame it on the concussion. Even that is pushing the time frame. Unless something shows up on the CT scan, her injury isn't bad enough to cause this type of amnesia and especially for it to hang on this long.

"I talked to a psychiatrist friend in Lubbock a few minutes ago. She's going to come down in a couple of days and examine Sunni. She'd come tomorrow but she's giving a seminar. If the tests don't give us a sound medical reason for the amnesia, she thinks it may be dissociative amnesia caused by trauma or stress."

"Like the trauma of being lost?"

"Possibly. You said you think she was on the Rocking K most of the time?"

"Had to be. I called the ranch on the way to town to see if she'd been camping in the far pasture. That would have explained why no one was looking for her. But no one there knew anything about her. She said she'd followed the creek since she woke up yesterday morning. It crosses onto my land about a mile from where I found her. The creek runs right through the middle of Caleb's land with twists and turns along the way. In that area, the ranch is fifteen miles across one way and about ten miles across the other. The sad thing is that a couple of times, she was probably within a mile of a house but couldn't see it."

"One thing is crucial, no matter what kind of amnesia this is," said the doctor. "We need to provide Sunni with a supportive environment that gives her a sense of safety."

"Lying in a hospital room won't accomplish that."

"Precisely." Doc leaned forward, pinning Jake with his gaze. "Her face lit up like a lightbulb when she saw you. When I mentioned a possible brain injury, she calmed down when you touched her." He grinned and leaned back, relaxing again. "Even the monitors picked up on it — pulse and respiratory rate slowed about two seconds after you put your hand on her shoulder.

"She feels safe with you, Jake. It's probably natural since you found her, but you also have a way of making people feel protected. Always have. Sunni needs that reassurance right now. She trusts you."

"I don't know, Doc. I wouldn't make a very good nurse."

"If everything checks out okay, you won't need to. She'll just need rest. Dr. Smith may suggest something different after she talks to Sunni, but for now, having her stay at your place seems like the best idea. Besides, Lynda will be there to help watch over her."

Jake stared at the floor. He didn't want to be responsible for her. Didn't want something happening to her on his watch. He didn't want emotional involvement or risk being hurt.

But he couldn't walk away and leave her to fend for herself, leave her to the mercy of strangers. He thought of her courage, her smile, her faith. How she brought out a gentleness in him that he thought he'd lost.

And the way she felt in his arms.

"She needs you," Doc said quietly.

He looked at the doctor and stood. "All right. Besides, Lynda would shoot me if I said no."

"Yes, she probably would." The doctor downed the rest of the coffee, tossed the foam cup in the garbage and walked from the room.

Jake followed and glanced down the hallway, remembering Sunni's wobbly smile. Maybe in some way he needed her, too.

Solitude was highly overrated anyway.

CHAPTER THREE

Two days later, Sunni sat curled up in the corner of the couch at Jake's, wearing a powder-pink knit T-shirt and matching summer-weight cotton sweatpants. His aunt had shown up at the hospital the day before with a complete set of new clothes, explaining that she owned a women's clothing store.

Sunni had considered that kind, but when she got to the house, she found over a week's worth of new clothes in the closet and dresser of the guest room. Everything from socks and undies to jeans and blouses. All a perfect fit. Most of the tops were a simple style in cool cotton knit, either sleeveless or short sleeved. A couple were a little fancier, crinkly cotton with pretty embroidery. She was amazed at Lynda's generosity and impressed with her knack for picking flattering styles and colors.

Jake's good friends and neighbors, Caleb

Kincaid and his sister, Megan Morrison, had come by shortly after she arrived the previous morning, from the hospital. They owned the Rocking K Ranch. They had been in Houston visiting relatives and had started home when Jake called them after he found her. They seemed nice, their concern for her genuine, not simply worried that she would sue them because she had been hurt on their land.

She certainly had no intention of trying to get any money out of them. Since they had no idea who she was, she didn't see how they could be blamed for her getting lost and hurt on their property.

Jake and the sheriff were holed up in Jake's office down the hall, doing something on the computer. Lynda was in the kitchen, quietly humming to herself as she baked a cake. She'd told her it was a welcome-home-from-the-hospital dessert, but Sunni suspected the treat was meant just as much to impress the sheriff. Which was fine with her. She already owed these kind people more than she could ever repay. As soon as her concussion healed and her strength returned, she'd help out as much as possible.

If she stayed.

She supposed that would be determined

by the psychiatrist sitting in the brown tweed swivel rocker directly across from her. Dr. Smith, a woman in her mid-forties, had arrived promptly at nine o'clock. They had been talking for a couple of hours.

Sunni wondered if her sympathy was real or merely a professional mask. Did she believe Sunni was telling the truth and the amnesia was real? Or would the doctor keep smiling and nodding and taking notes, then march down the hall to Jake's office and tell him and the sheriff that she was a bold-faced liar and probably a gangster's moll.

An image popped into her mind of a slinky, long-legged blonde — definitely not her — hanging on the arm of a machine-gun-toting mob boss. *Maybe I am certifiably nuts,* she thought with a quiet sigh.

Dr. Smith looked up, her pen poised above her notepad. "What are you thinking?"

Sunni gave her a wry shrug. "I'm wondering what *you're* thinking, which somehow led to a mental image of a gangster's moll."

The doctor laughed and rested her hand and the pen on the pad. "You or me?"

"Neither. She was blond, but a whole lot taller than me. Some movie star, I think, but I couldn't tell you who."

"So you do have some memories other

than typical everyday things such as liking your tea sweet and your bacon crisp."

Sunni nodded, then frowned. "But it's just snippets."

"Give me some examples."

Sunni glanced down the hall and lowered her voice. "The day Jake found me, I was looking at his eyes and wondered if they were always the deep blue of the Pacific Ocean on a bright sunny morning."

The doctor grinned. "They are gorgeous, aren't they. So you've seen the Pacific Ocean?"

"I must have, but I can't remember anything specific."

"Perhaps a picture in a magazine?"

"It seems more vivid, like something I've actually experienced."

"Anything else?"

She told her about remembering a partial phrase from the Cowboy Santa song and "seeing" the dashboard of her car.

Dr. Smith was making notes again. "Anything on the dashboard to tell you what kind of car it was?" she asked casually.

"No. But I have the impression that it was roomy. Definitely not a compact." She considered telling the doctor how she'd felt the first day at the house. The security that came from Jake holding her hand and feeling as if she'd experienced such a thing before with someone else. She decided against mentioning it. Somehow it seemed too personal.

"The nurse said you had a nightmare while you were in the hospital. Can you remember it?"

Jake strolled into the living room and sat down on the other end of the couch, resting his arm along the back of it. "You didn't mention having a nightmare."

Sunni resisted the impulse to scoot over beside him. She would have kept the dream to herself, but Rita Mae Nash, her hospital roommate, had buzzed for the nurse. She didn't doubt that the woman's intentions were good. To hear Rita Mae tell it, Sunni had been thrashing around on the bed, moaning as if she were terrified.

And she had been. "It was scary and all jumbled up, like two horror movies scrambled together. I didn't want to think about it. I figured it was just because I'd been lost."

"Do you mind telling me about it?" the doctor asked quietly.

So she could analyze it? Did psychiatrists really do that? "I was running across the ranch and wild animals, kind of like wolves, were chasing me. One of them howled, the same noise I heard the night before you found me."

"Coyotes. We don't have any wolves around here."

"I wouldn't know the difference from the howl. They seemed awfully close, but I never saw them."

"Except in your dream," said Dr. Smith.

Sunni nodded. "I was running, scrambling through the brush, scraping against mesquite branches, falling down a couple of times. They changed back and forth between the wolves and a giant cat, like a cougar. It opened its mouth to snarl or roar or whatever they do, but what came out was a scream." A shiver swept over her.

"You may have heard a mountain lion the first night when you were so disoriented. That's what we call cougars in this part of the country. There are a couple that come through here on occasion." Jake slid across the sofa to her side, resting his arm around her shoulders.

She glanced up at him, giving him a tiny smile of thanks. "Maybe. Suddenly, I was in a city. Paved streets, sidewalks, a lot of commotion." Her heart began to ache, not the same agony as when she had awakened, but still with a pain that went soul deep. Somehow, she knew this was a memory, not merely part of the dream.

"I was kneeling on the sidewalk, holding a man in my arms. He was hurt, with blood all over his chest, and I kept screaming for someone to help me."

Dr. Smith shifted in her chair, assuming a slightly more relaxed position, setting her pen down again.

Trying to put her more at ease? It didn't help.

"What happened to him?"

"I don't know. I woke up."

"How did you feel when you woke up?"

"Like my heart was being ripped out." Tears filled her eyes, and she squeezed them shut.

"And now?"

"Heartache." She looked up at the doctor. "It seems too real to only be a dream." Her voice broke, and Jake's arm tightened around her shoulders. A tear trickled down her cheek, and she angrily wiped it away. Why couldn't she remember? She wanted to scream in frustration. "How can I hurt so badly for someone and not even know who he is?"

Dr. Smith studied her for a minute. "Dreams can be very powerful, seem very real, but still be nothing more than a dream. However, it's also possible that you are remembering an actual event."

Jake reached over to the coffee table and picked up a box of tissues, handing them to Sunni. As she wiped her eyes and blew her nose, the sheriff joined them, sitting down in a big brown, gold and rust geometric-patterned chair that matched the sofa.

The psychiatrist closed her notebook and glanced at him. "Sunni is suffering from a textbook case of amnesia."

The sheriff's eyebrows went up, then his eyes narrowed as he looked at Sunni. She could easily imagine what he was thinking. Textbook case — so she's read up on it and knows exactly how to act.

"I believe it's real," said Dr. Smith.

Sunni almost cried again in relief. "Because I hit my head?"

"No, I don't think that has much to do with it. I believe you are suffering from dissociative amnesia which is caused by a psychological disturbance rather than a physical one. In this type of amnesia, the loss involves the autobiographical memory — who you are, where you've been, what you thought or felt, etc.

"The lab results ruled out toxins or drugs. And it's very rare for this type of head injury to cause general amnesia, if at all. My guess — and it's only a guess at this point — is that being lost and fearing for your life brought back the emotional trauma of something that happened before."

"The injured man," said Jake.

"Yes. He may have been a stranger, and Sunni's pain and grief result from her inability to help him." She turned her attention to Sunni again. "It's more likely, however, that you knew him, possibly that he was very dear to you. Being hurt and lost not only brought back the trauma of that first experience, but added so much psychological stress that your mind has blocked your memories. It's a protective device, a way of hiding from the emotional pain."

"But I hurt anyway."

"Yes, but that's a good sign. It suggests that you will regain your memory."

Jake frowned and voiced Sunni's thoughts before she could. "Suggests? You mean she might not?"

"It's possible, but I think eventually almost everything will come back to you. You obviously had a concussion, which might cause you to lose what happened around the time of the injury."

"Which is why I don't remember much about that first night?" asked Sunni. "I don't have any blanks after I woke up the next morning."

"That's right."

"So even if she gets her memory back, she might not be able to tell us what happened to her?" asked Jake.

"There's a chance, yes. All we can do is wait and see."

"It will be soon, though, won't it?" asked Sunni.

"There's no way to know," said the doctor. "It could be days or weeks —" she met Sunni's gaze "— or months. You should keep having little flashes, which eventually will add up until you know something about yourself. That may help you discover other things, connect the dots so to speak. Then one day, everything else will suddenly come back. It's likely to be somewhat overwhelming."

"Is there any way to speed it along?" asked the sheriff.

"We could try hypnosis or drug-facilitated interviews, but I don't like to do either unless I absolutely have to. Memories recalled in that way may not be accurate. We would have to obtain external corroboration, which may be difficult to do. It might only confuse her, plus those techniques can cause extreme anxiety."

Sunni grimaced. "Thanks. I have enough

anxiety already."

"In this type of amnesia, returning to the place associated with the memory loss sometimes restores it. But it doesn't always work." Dr. Smith glanced at the sheriff, then focused on Jake. "Do you know where she may have been?"

"Just a general idea. We had a thunderstorm late on the afternoon I found her. It wiped out her trail. I didn't have time to go back out there before the rain hit. We know she followed the creek and climbed out of a canyon. But there are half-a-dozen canyons on that side of the Rocking K, and the creek splits off a few times, too."

"We've searched all around the Rocking K, Jake's ranch, the farms next to them and along the highways for an abandoned car," said the sheriff.

Sunni looked at him in surprise. That was news to her, though she should have known he wasn't just twiddling his thumbs waiting for her memory to come back. Jake had been gone most of the previous day, but she hadn't known what he had been doing. She was aware that he and the sheriff had checked every database available but came up empty-handed. "Could you have missed it?"

"Not likely. Jake and the Rocking K

cowboys have driven all over both ranches. And Caleb called in the chopper pilot he uses to help with the roundup. They've flown over every acre of his ranch, and Jake's, too. My deputies have covered the highways and side roads. All the neighbors have thoroughly checked their places, too."

"How could it just disappear?" asked Sunni. "And why would I stop in the first place?"

"Folks stop along the highway all the time. It's a scenic two-lane road, not an interstate." The sheriff crossed his ankles. "Some picnic at the rest stop. It's just a covered table with a few trees around it, but it's a nice place to take a break on a long trip. Others rummage through old houses along the road looking for antiques or collectibles. Take the glass doorknobs or the old-fashioned locks." He snorted. "They've even started pulling out the window frames, don't care if they have glass in them or not."

Sunni made a face. "I hope I'm not like that."

"Lots of folks wander around pastures looking for arrowheads or birds or wildflowers. Or stop to take pictures. There's some mighty pretty scenery around here."

"I like birds and flowers." Sunni smiled at the sheriff. "And the scenery. But if I stopped for any of those reasons, why wouldn't my car still be there?"

The sheriff's expression grew serious. "It's possible you were abducted and left out there. But Doc said there was no indication that you'd been abused and that your injuries are consistent with falling down the cliff as you supposed. You haven't shown up on any of the missing persons databases, so I think someone intentionally trying to harm you isn't likely. Not impossible, but it's a long shot.

"We've had a rash of car thefts in the area, both here and in neighboring counties during the past six months. My current theory is that you were just stretching your legs a bit, taking a little walk through a pasture to see what it was like or look at the flowers. You wandered a little farther than you'd planned, got disoriented with the directions, became dehydrated and fell. You left your car beside the highway, and it proved too great a temptation for somebody."

"For now, that's the most plausible theory we have," added Jake. "A rancher in the next county had his pickup stolen that way. Stopped along the road and walked out into the pasture to check on a windmill. When he got back to the road, his truck was gone. Fortunately, he had his cell phone clipped to his belt, so he called his wife to pick him up."

The psychiatrist put her notebook and pen in a briefcase and withdrew a small book with red roses on the cover. She handed it to Sunni. "As other memories come back to you, jot them down in here. If you are aware of what triggered them, note that, too. Keeping a record and sharing them with someone may help you recover other things."

She gave both Sunni and Jake her business cards. "This is my cell number. Call me day or night if you need me. Otherwise I'll come back to see you in a couple of days." When she stood, Jake and the sheriff did, too.

"Thank you for driving all the way out here." Sunni started to get up, but the doctor motioned for her to stay seated.

"Glad to do it," she said with a grin. "Yours is a fascinating case, and it gives me a chance to get away from the office. I'm long overdue for a visit with James and Beth — Dr. Hampton and his wife. I'll be staying with them through the weekend."

"Talking to you has helped. I'm not quite as anxious as I was."

"Good. That means I'm doing my job." Dr. Smith glanced from Lynda standing in the kitchen door to Jake and the sheriff. "Doc Hampton and these folks will take good care of you."

"I know they will."

Sunni watched the sheriff walk the doctor out to her car. "Do you think he believes her? And me?"

"Looks like it." Jake sat back down and turned so he could look at her. "Being suspicious about everything and everybody goes with the job. If you aren't that way when you first become a lawman, you soon learn to be. Often things aren't as they first seem to be."

Frowning, she searched his eyes. "Do you think I'm making all this up?"

"No. The evidence supports your story, as does Dr. Smith's opinion."

Sunni tried to ignore the little zing of disappointment. It was wrong to expect him to simply believe her without any proof. If she were in his shoes — or boots, as it were — she'd have been skeptical, too. She pondered that thought for a minute, realizing it was true.

He tipped his head, studying her face. "I see wheels turning. . . ."

"It seems I may have a suspicious, or at least skeptical, nature, too. If I were in your position, I'd want proof."

"I expect most people would." He took hold of her hand, rubbing his thumb lightly across the back of it. "But just so you know, I never had any serious doubts about you or your story."

"None?"

His smile was slow and lazy. "Nope. I figured if you were that good an actress, you wouldn't be stuck out here by yourself. You'd have a whole Hollywood entourage tagging along." He leaned back against the couch, his arm touching hers. "A diamond-bedazzled starlet traipsing across the prairie in high heels and a leopard-skin miniskirt —"

"Me in leopard skin?"

"Yep, and you're chewing gum, too."

"Bubble gum." Sunni grinned up at him.

He chuckled and nodded. "Blowing big bubbles. You're followed by a brush-wielding hairdresser, a flunky misting you with water from a spray bottle and a high-powered agent ranting and raving into a cell phone."

Laughing, Sunni rested her head against his shoulder. "Thanks, both for not doubting me and for the laugh."

"Glad to oblige."

She looked down at their clasped hands, wondering what life would be like if her memory never returned.

For a heartbeat she almost wished it wouldn't.

CHAPTER FOUR

The first three days after Sunni returned to Jake's ranch, he had stayed around, mainly painting the outside of the house. She hadn't seen much of him then because all she seemed to do was sleep. After she perked up enough to camp out on the couch most of the day, he went back to more of his regular work. He still had dropped by the house every few hours to check on her, especially if she was by herself.

Lynda had stayed home from her store until noon every day for the past week, and Megan had stopped by three times to visit. But now that Sunni was pretty much back to normal — physically anyway — everyone seemed to have abandoned her. She was annoyed with herself for feeling that way. She appreciated all the care they had given her and didn't expect them to babysit her, but she needed something to do.

Lynda had gone to work around nine, and

Jake had left even earlier for parts unknown. She had persuaded them to let her do the breakfast dishes, which took ten minutes to accomplish. She would gladly have done more, but Jake's once-a-month cleaning lady had been there the day before.

Sunni read the Bible for awhile, drawing strength from Jesus' promise *that if you abide in Me, I will abide in you.* "Help me to live for You, Lord, to live in You," she prayed fervently. "Thank You for Your love and protection, for all the provision You've given me. Fill me with Your love, let me always be grateful for all You've done for me."

Worshipping God quietly, she prayed for His blessing on everyone she knew — all fifteen people, counting the doctors, nurses and technicians that she'd met. She prayed for the family and friends she didn't know, hoping there were some.

She worked on Jake's computer, as she had done the previous afternoon, research-ing states and cities, hoping something would spark her memory. She'd started on the West Coast because Jake said she didn't have a Southern or East Coast accent. And there was that thought — or memory — of the Pacific Ocean on a clear day. So far, she'd covered half of California and come up empty-handed.

Being at the computer for more than an hour gave her a headache. She didn't know if it was a remnant of the concussion or if she was trying to cram too much information into her poor addled brain.

Now, she was down to watching television. Saturday wasn't any better than the weekday stuff, unless you liked golf, bass fishing or restoring old cars. Stopping on a cartoon channel, she smiled as a coyote tried to outsmart a roadrunner. "Never going to happen, buddy." Part of another episode flashed through her mind, but it was gone as quickly as it appeared. "Guess I watched you guys when I was a kid."

During the past week, she had enjoyed some of the programs on the history channel or the ones about home projects. Except she didn't have a history. Or a home. And that depressed her.

She moved on to the weather channel. Thunderstorms hammered Tennessee and Kentucky again. Hot and dry in Texas.

Jake came in the back door, stopped in the kitchen for a drink of water and wandered into the living room. He was as handsome as ever in a purple-striped Western shirt. He looked at the weather map for a minute, listening to the forecast for Italy and France, then turned to her with a hint of a smile. "Planning a trip?"

"Not to faraway lands. Misplaced my passport." And everything else.

"Want to get out of here for a while?"

"Yes." Sunni turned off the television and laid the remote on the coffee table. Hopping up from the couch, she straightened her light lemon-yellow tank top. "Otherwise, I'm liable to start rearranging the furniture."

Jake glanced around the room. "What's wrong with the way I have it?"

"Nothing. But I'm bored silly. It's either redecorate your house or clean cabinets. Redecorating would be more fun."

"But the cabinets probably need cleaning out. No telling what you'd find."

"Today I really need a change of scenery." She headed toward her bedroom. "Let me get my shoes. I've already discovered the stickers in your yard."

When she came back into the living room carrying her shoes and socks, Jake was sitting in the rocker. "Ventured out barefoot, huh?"

She sat down on the end of the sofa and pulled on her socks. "I've discovered that I enjoy going barefoot, but nobody warned me about grass burrs. Lynda told me what they were after I got one stuck in my foot."

"Sorry. That probably means you haven't been around here long. It also tells me that what knowledge you do have about the area likely came from reading about it, or maybe seeing something on television."

"We've already established by my non-accent that I'm not from Texas." She slid her foot into the shoe and tied the laces. He grinned as she picked up the other shoe. "What?"

"I only said that you don't have a Texas accent. Or one that's distinguishable from a certain area of the country, such as the South or New York or Boston. I didn't say that you don't have an accent." His voice took on an exaggerated drawl. "To folks around here, you sound a mite funny."

Sunni tugged the bow on the second shoelace tight and stood. "Reckon I need to start talkin' Texan, so I kin fit right in."

Jake laughed as he stood and draped his arm around her shoulders, steering her toward the back door. Licorice followed them. "You'll pick it up soon enough without trying. Most folks do."

"Where are we going?"

"To the hardware store. I need to get some nails and new hinges for the barn door." He looked down at her. "Are you any good with a hammer?"

"I don't know. But I'm willing to try."

"I was just kidding. I don't expect you to work." His expression grew serious. "Both Doc Hampton and Dr. Smith told you to take it easy for a couple of weeks."

"I'll go bonkers if I don't have something to do besides watch television."

"You can tag along with me if you want to."

"I'd like that. I haven't seen much of your ranch." And she missed him when he wasn't around.

When they went out the back door, Sunni noticed that he didn't bother to lock it. She supposed he didn't have to worry much about thieves out here, but locking the door seemed normal to her.

"You're thinking again."

She glanced up to find him watching her. "I would have locked the door automatically. So I must live in the city."

"Not necessarily. A lot of folks in Coyote Springs lock their doors. I figure there's not much to worry about out here during the day. Half the time I'm working close by anyway. The house is far enough off the highway that nobody wanders back here unless they know me." He opened the extended cab door on the light blue pickup so Licorice could hop inside to the back seat,

76

then held open Sunni's door. "Need a boost?"

The thought of him lifting her up to the seat was appealing, but the truck had running boards and handles to help climb inside. If she said yes to his assistance, he'd think she wasn't as strong as she felt. Or he'd realize she just wanted to feel his hands around her waist. "No thanks, I can climb in okay."

He waited until she was settled, shut the door and walked around to the driver's side. As he fastened his seat belt, he glanced to see that she had put hers on. Licorice sat mostly on one side of the back seat looking out the window.

They drove toward the highway, past cows grazing in the open pasture. Jake slowed down, checking them over.

Sunni wondered if she'd always thought cows were pretty. These certainly were. "They look healthy and happy."

"Happy cows?" The corners of Jake's eyes crinkled when he smiled. "I suppose they are. They've had good grass this spring. This will hold them for a while. Then I'll move them into a field of Sudan sorghum. Move them in too soon and they can get poisoned, but if you wait until it's long enough, they can munch on it for quite a while."

There were several different kinds of cattle in the pasture. She didn't know what they were, except that a couple were similar to some Longhorns she'd seen in a movie earlier in the week. "Do you raise specific breeds?"

"Herefords, Black Angus, Texas Longhorns and a couple of different crosses." Jake stopped the truck. Some of the cows looked at them expectantly. "The ones that are reddish-brown with white faces, chest and legs, like that one moseying this way, are Herefords. The solid black are Black Angus, and that little black calf with the white face is a Hereford-Black Angus cross called a black baldy."

"She's cute." Sunni unbuckled her seat belt and leaned up in the seat, resting her arm on the dashboard. A little multicolored reddish-brown, white-and-brown calf raced by the black baldy, prompting a chase. "What's the one that looks like abstract art?"

Jake laughed, glancing at her before turning back to the cattle. "That's a Longhorn-Hereford cross. First-time Hereford mamas do better if the papa is either an Angus or a Longhorn. They produce smaller babies, which makes calving — the birth — easier."

She pointed to a buckskin-colored cow

with horns about two feet long on each side of her head. Her baby was mostly white with brown and buckskin patches. "She must be a Texas Longhorn."

"That's right. Purebred. So is her calf. The demand for Longhorns is growing so I'm working on increasing the purebreds in my herd." He shifted the truck into gear. "I have some Longhorn calves leased out for roping and cutting competitions."

Sunni settled back in the seat, fastening her seat belt. "How do you get a rope over those big horns?"

"It's tricky. Need a real big one." His eyes twinkled as he drove around a pothole in the road. It would be easy to get used to hanging out with Jake Trayner. "The calves are eight to ten months old. At that age, the horns are about six inches past their ears. They're quick and agile, which makes them perfect for cutting horse competitions. They don't get tired easy, either, and they're intelligent. I think they like trying to outsmart those cutting horses."

"Is that where the horse and rider try to separate a calf from a herd? I saw an ad for something like that yesterday. But it looked as if the horse was doing all the work."

"That's the whole idea. It really is more about the horse, though the rider has to know what he's doing, too. Once he — or she — has decided which calf to cut and has the horse lined up on it, the rider lowers his hands to loosen the reins and lets the horse go to work. It's big-time competition now, but cutting horses, mostly quarter horses, have been used on ranches for ages."

He drove across the metal cattle guard in the barbed wire fence separating the ranch from the highway. After checking to make sure no cars were coming, he pulled out onto the road.

"I probably won't sell any of my calves this year. Though this land has been in the family for generations, I didn't run any cattle while I was with the Highway Patrol or the Rangers. Didn't have the time. But I socked my money away, figuring I'd move back here someday. That happened a little sooner than I'd planned. I only started ranching again a little over a year ago and need to build up the herd.

"I have them split into three different pastures, about thirty head in each, counting the new calves. Next week, we'll be moving one group over to the pasture where I found you."

He'd told her that his parents had died when he was twenty, victims of a drunk driver. It had prompted him to go into law enforcement. The day before, she'd done an Internet search on the Texas Rangers, learning that few people made it into that elite force. He had gone far in his career. Why had he quit? Although curious, she sensed it wasn't a topic that would be easily discussed.

"When did your family settle here?"

"My great-great-grandpa, Colin Fraser, was a Scottish immigrant who came to the area with a herd of Longhorns in 1879. There was grass as far as the eye could see."

"That's about what it is now except for some mesquite trees and an occasional windmill."

"And fences. There weren't any back then, just wide-open range. Free grass. Men came out with their herds, found a piece of land they liked and claimed it. Usually they bought just enough acreage to secure water, either at a spring or along a creek, then let the cattle graze the surrounding area."

"What if someone else wanted it?"

"There were some squabbles, mostly handled in the courts. A few were resolved with six-shooters. If they were smart, like my great-great-grandpa, in addition to land they bought, they leased acreage from the state. Grandpa Colin had a herd out here and one near where they built Coyote

Springs when the railroad came through in 1881. He was one of the town founders, in fact.

"With the ability to ship the cattle instead of having to drive them long distances to market, more ranchers moved in. Pretty soon folks started fencing their land with barbed wire — or *bob war* as it's called around here. They could improve the herds and take better care of them during a rough winter or drought."

When Licorice stuck his face between the bucket seats and nudged Sunni on the shoulder, she reached back and scratched him under the chin. "How did a Scottish immigrant wind up as a rancher in Texas?"

"In 1873, when he was nineteen, he accompanied four Aberdeen-Angus bulls from Scotland to Victoria, Kansas. They were the first Angus cattle to be brought to the United States. His employer, Sir George MacPherson-Grant of Ballindalloch, Scotland, wanted to establish a colony of wealthy British stockmen in Kansas. He imported the first Aberdeen-Angus bulls to the U.S., and Colin came along to take care of them.

"But the lure of the Wild West was too strong for Colin. After a year, he hooked up with a Texas cattleman, learned the business and bought a small herd of Longhorns.

They were the only breed in Texas at the time.

"Grandpa Colin was one of the first to bring Angus cattle to Texas around 1885. He started with one bull that he bred with Longhorns. Over the following five years, he imported four bulls and twenty cows directly from Ballindalloch and slowly established a purebred Angus herd. Most of the Angus I have now are descendants of his original herd."

He was quiet, sadness replacing the animation that had been in his countenance a moment before. "When I quit ranching, I sold the Angus herd to Caleb with the understanding that he would keep the bulls and cows until I decided to buy them back. He could sell all the calves he wanted to. I still cried the day I moved them off this land. I felt as if I was letting down everybody who ever owned this ranch."

"But you have them back now. That has to feel good."

He smiled, visibly shaking off his momentary melancholy. "Yeah, it does. I don't intend to boot those poor critters — or myself — off this land ever again."

They passed a small church with a cemetery next to it. "That's been here for a while," said Sunni, twisting around in the seat to look at it longer.

"Since the 1890's. It's the Kincaid Community Church. This area was named after Caleb's great-great-grandfather, Jordan Kincaid. He came here in 1881, when they were first planning the town. He was a successful businessman from Galveston. He opened a bank in Coyote Springs and then established the Rocking K Ranch."

"The church building looks in good shape. Does anyone still use it?"

"Every Sunday morning. Lynda's been attending there ever since she moved back to Coyote Springs, even though she normally lives in town."

"But you don't?"

"No."

Though the little church looked interesting, Sunni wanted to see where Jake went. Okay, she admitted to herself, she'd rather just go with Jake. "Do you go somewhere in town?"

Jake kept his eyes on the road. "No."

His tone made it clear that he didn't want to talk about it. When he'd found her at the creek and she'd been talking about God watching out for her, he had said that having faith wasn't strange. But that didn't mean he was a believer. The thought that he might not know the love of Jesus made her sad. How could anyone go through life without God's guidance and strength, without the assurance of redemption?

The landscape began to change, still mostly rangeland but with more green fields here and there. After a few miles, the mix equaled out with as much land in cultivation as in pasture. "What are they growing?"

"It's cotton. It's the main cash crop in this part of Texas."

"I hope they don't ever quit raising it." Sunni smoothed her fingers over the leg of her jeans. "It's more comfortable than anything else."

Jake slanted a glance in her direction. "Are you saying that just because everything Lynda brought you is made from cotton or is it a memory?"

Sunni wrinkled her forehead, trying to decide. "Some of both, I think. I'm very pleased with all the clothes Lynda gave me. But I'm positive I don't like synthetics, such as polyester and nylon." She suddenly pictured a little girl wearing a pretty pair of blue-flowered pajamas, but the child's neck and arms were red and itching like mad. Wide-eyed, she looked at Jake. "Nylon gives me hives."

"You remember something specific?"

She nodded. "A pair of nylon pajamas trimmed in lace. But within minutes after I put them on, I broke out in a horrible rash. I was ten years old."

"Do you remember what you looked like at ten?"

"Pigtails and red and blotchy skin from the pj's." She closed her eyes, straining for something more. Sighing in disappointment, she rested her head on the back of the seat. "That's it."

"It's something to jot down in your notebook. At least now you know you need to avoid nylon. A lot of us don't like polyester. It's like wearing a plastic bag."

"True, but it doesn't wrinkle," she said with a forced smile, injecting a light note in her voice.

"Yeah, but you'll never catch me in a leisure suit."

Her gaze skimmed over his Western shirt, well-worn jeans and boots. "I can't imagine anyone around here wearing leisure suits even when they were in style."

"A few city guys did." He grinned and touched the brake lightly as a car pulled out up the road. "The mayor of Coyote Springs for one. There's a picture of him hanging in city hall. He didn't win election to a second term."

"Because of his clothes?"

"The duds probably didn't help. Mostly, he turned out to be a lousy mayor."

Ten minutes later, they arrived in Coyote Springs, population four thousand thirteen according to the sign at the city limits.

"I'll give you the grand tour," said Jake, halting at the Main Street stop sign. An old ornate courthouse with a huge lawn on three sides sat right in front of them. A modern building, apparently the jail, was next to it on the right. Offices and shops were located on the opposite side of the street all around the square. "This is down-town, otherwise known as the courthouse square or city square."

A quick glance revealed that a street intersected Main on both the east and west sides of the courthouse. She assumed there would be one coming in from the north as well. According to the sign at the intersection, the highway they were on was also called South Spruce Street. "I didn't see this on my trips to and from the hospital."

"When we came through here, you were asleep both times."

He turned right, passing the contemporary-style National Bank Building, an insurance office and a real estate office. Turning left, he followed Main Street around the square.

Sunni noted the stores but also studied the architecture. Only the bank and the jail appeared to have been built in the past twenty years. Many of the buildings were made of brick and several had false fronts, giving the impression of a second story. "Are these really as old as they look?"

"Almost all of them were built between 1881 and 1910. It's a point of city pride that they've been able to keep them in good shape."

The east side of the square held city hall, the Coyote Springs Police Department and Silver Spur Antiques, which Jake said had been a saloon in the early days. A sign at the intersection of East First Street and Main pointed to more parking behind the buildings. Lynda's clothing store, the Classy Lady, was on the other side of First, along with the Coyote Springs Drug and the Sunrise Café.

He turned left again. Nielson Furniture, Belle's Florist, Hargrove Title Insurance, the *Coyote Springs Guardian* newspaper and an attorney's office were on the north side, along with a couple of empty buildings. North Spruce Street dissected the block between the newspaper office and the attorney's. "The *Guardian* has been here since the town's beginning. They have every one of their weekly newspapers on microfilm."

On the west side of the square, Kendrick Hardware was on one corner of West First and Main, with the electric company office on the other corner. There were several empty storefronts on either side of them.

Jake started another loop around the courthouse, past Dot's Beauty Shop, the Uptown Café and a few more empty buildings on the south side before they drove by the bank again. He took East First, past Newcastle's Feed and Seed, Anderson's Farm Implement Company and Grayson Lumberyard, all with ample parking. A block down was the Quick Stop gas station and convenience store. Several empty buildings dotted the street.

He drove four blocks farther to the Farmer's Co-op Cotton Gin and pulled off in front of the big, tall metal building. Though closed, there were bits of white fluffy cotton tangled in the weeds around it. Adjacent was a huge open area, covering several blocks.

"When they're harvesting cotton in late fall and early winter, this part of the yard will be full of modules of cotton waiting to be ginned." He pointed to the other side of the open space. "After it's processed, the bales go over there. They're sold and hauled off to various factories across the country. The seeds are taken out during ginning and are sent to a mill where they press out the oil and process the remaining seed into various forms. Most ranchers, including me, use cottonseed cake — a pellet of cottonseed meal — to supplement the grass for the cattle."

He gave her a few minutes to look over the gin, then turned around and headed back toward downtown. "The library and fire station are a block from the square on West First. The schools are in the residential neighborhoods. The dentist, doctors and hospital are on the north side of town."

"I remember that. Aren't they close to the freeway?"

Jake nodded. "That's right. I-20. Another attorney, two gas stations, an auto-parts store and a couple of fast-food places are out that way, too. Taylor's Grocery is on Third Street where they have plenty of parking. The funeral home is on Fifth and various churches are scattered all over town as, I'm sure, are some other places I'm not thinking of. The Livestock Auction, a well driller, and a car-repair shop are in the west end. Basically a typical West Texas town."

"Do you know everybody?"

"A lot of them, but not all. The clerks at the grocery store can probably give you the rundown on just about anybody in town and most of the county."

"Even you?" Sunni smiled at him, her eyes twinkling impishly. His insides turned to mush, and he almost missed the empty parking space in front of the hardware store. He hit the brakes and whipped into the spot, practically throwing Licorice into his lap. "That smile of yours is dangerous."

Her eyes widened all innocent-like and twinkled even more. It was a good thing he still had on his seat belt. Better that Licorice was wedged between them, his front feet shuffling precariously on the center console as he tried to get unstuck. Otherwise, Jake might have leaned over and kissed her right there on Main Street.

And caused an uproar. She was his house-guest. Well, his and Lynda's. He was supposed to be taking care of her, helping her deal with her amnesia, watching out for her. Not embarrass her or give folks more reason for fence talk.

Lynda had already warned them that the minute Sunni was dismissed from the hospital, Rita Mae Nash had practically set the phone lines on fire spreading the word about Sunni. The hospital administrator had finally taken the phone out of her room because she kept the line tied up so long. Rita kept it up after she got home, declaring that the story of a sweet young woman with a *gen-u-ine* case of amnesia was even more interesting than her gallbladder surgery.

Nor should he be thinking about her in a romantic way. She was off-limits until they found out who she was. He couldn't imagine a woman as sweet as Sunni not being married or at least involved with someone. But if she were, wouldn't the guy have reported her missing by now? Jake checked the missing persons databases every night after Sunni went to bed.

It didn't matter. She was off-limits, period. He could be a friend, that's all. No entanglements. He was no good at relationships — caring for someone only brought pain. He already had enough heartache and guilt to last a lifetime.

Jake unfastened his seat belt and gave Licorice a gentle shove, helping him into the back seat. The dog snorted and grumbled, wiggling around to get settled as Jake hit the electric buttons and lowered the windows. With one last snort, Licorice stuck his nose out the back window, sniffing the air.

"Don't be surprised if somebody makes a comment about you or the amnesia." Jake hoped if anybody said anything that they would be kind. He'd hate to be arrested for punching some jerk or throttling a leaky-mouthed woman.

"I'll be okay. I'm bound to be a curiosity."

"If anybody bothers you, you tell me."

Sunni unfastened her seat belt and looked around, left and right, even out the back window.

Frowning, Jake touched her arm. "What are you doing?"

"Looking for your horse. How can you come riding to my rescue without a horse?"

There was that smile again, the merriment dancing in her eyes. He sensed that she wasn't making fun of him. She was just enjoying the moment. Enjoying him.

He had one foot in quicksand, and the other was sliding closer by the second. He needed to get out of the truck pronto. Instead he leaned a little closer, running his finger across a strand of blond hair lying on the headrest. Silky. "I already did that," he said quietly.

"Yeah, you did." Her voice was soft and tender.

There went the other foot.

"Jake . . . yoo-hoo!" A redhead hurrying

down the sidewalk sent him jerking back and straightening in his seat. "Don't you go running off, Jake Trayner," she called, waving her hand.

"Who's that?" whispered Sunni.

"Penny Webster Wilson. My old high school flame. At least she was until Gerald Wilson moved to town. She took one look at him and said *adios, amigo.*" He caught Sunni's searching glance and smiled. "I didn't mind. She's nice but she hollered like that back then, too."

Sunni's giggle had him still smiling when his old girlfriend stepped up to his window. "Mornin', Penny."

"Good morning." Penny gave him a quick grin then zeroed in on the passenger seat. "You must be Sunni."

"That's right." Sunni's tone was polite but cautious.

"We heard all about you at the garden club last night — at least Rita Mae's version of the story about ten times removed. Of course, who knows how much it's changed, both in her telling and others' embellishments. It was the most interesting meeting we've had since Lila Graves was showing us how to burn the spines off prickly pear and set her house on fire."

"Take a breath, Penny." Jake rested his

arm along the open window.

She made a face at him, then chuckled. "I just wanted to meet you and tell you how glad I am that you're safe and sound. Do you really have amnesia?"

"Yes, I'm afraid so."

Jake glanced at Sunni. Was that a slight tremble in her voice? She looked composed, but she wasn't smiling.

Penny shook her head. "Bless your heart. That must be about the scariest thing ever." She patted Jake's arm affectionately. "But you couldn't be in better hands."

It was time to change the subject. "How's Gerald?"

"Oh, he's fine. Same dear Gerald. He and his crew are almost finished with the Graves's new house." She looked at Sunni again. "My husband is a carpenter, sometimes contractor. When he doesn't have a new house to build, he keeps busy doing remodeling jobs. He's the best in the county."

"That he is." Jake checked on Sunni out of the corner of his eye. He decided she was doing all right. "Lynda was disappointed that he couldn't oversee the remodeling on her house."

"Gerald was, too. He would have loved to tackle that old place. But he has two more jobs lined up when this one is done, and Lynda didn't want to wait that long."

"She couldn't. The old wiring needed to be replaced. She had a close call with a potential fire herself. Since that was being done, it made more sense to go ahead with the whole remodel. Now, if you'll excuse us, I need to go pick up a few things in the hardware store."

Penny stepped back. "I'm going into Kendrick's, too. Some plants I ordered came in."

Sunni climbed out of the pickup before Jake had a chance to go around and open her door. She met Penny on the sidewalk. "Do they have a good garden department?"

"A pretty decent one. Are you a gardener?"

"I don't know." Sunni shrugged. "Probably not. I don't remember anything about flowers except that I like them. Jake needs some to brighten up his yard."

He joined them on the sidewalk. "Things don't grow well around the house. It's not good dirt." At least that's what his mother always said. He hadn't given it a try. He'd never planted a flower in his life. "We could get some potted plants, but I wouldn't know what kind."

"Me, either." Sunni looked disappointed.

"I'll help you pick something out." Penny beamed. "Growing things — plants and kids — is my specialty."

"Great. You and Sunni go pick out whatever you want, and I'll get my stuff. But don't take too long. Licorice is gettin' hungry."

Both women laughed and hurried into the store, making a beeline for the garden department. Jake followed leisurely along behind them, watching as they chatted away. Penny said something to Sunni that made her grin and glance back at him. He winked and veered off to look for nails.

He refused to think about why seeing Sunni happy meant so much to him.

CHAPTER FIVE

After much discussion with Penny, Jake and Sunni settled on purchasing six large planters already filled with flowers. Instant color, a lot less work, and they were perfect for the yard.

They put two of the pots filled with yellow and orange dahlias, white daisies and some kind of ornamental grass by the front porch. The grass reminded him of some stuff he'd seen in the pasture, but he didn't mention it to the ladies.

They set the other planters on the patio along the screen porch. He moved aside the hand truck he'd used to cart the heavy planters, and they stood back to admire them. The flowers in one were predominately light blue with some red verbena and yellow something thrown into the mix. Another held dark purple petunias and red geraniums. He'd never thought about red and purple looking good together, but they did in a flowerpot. The third was a mix of pink geraniums, light purple bell-shaped flowers and a thick layer of plants with tiny white flowers that cascaded over the edge of the pot. The last one was a combination of bright red and yellow flowers.

Penny had named all the plants, but neither he nor Sunni could remember most of them. Penny had assured them that they really didn't have to know what they were. They just needed to water them before they wilted, give them a little fertilizer occasionally and trim off the dead flowers.

"That one needs to go to the left a little bit more." Sunni pointed to the container of red and purple that sat to the left of the door.

"Remind me not to let you rearrange the furniture," he grumbled with a grin. He'd already given his back a workout lifting the heavy containers off the truck. Kneeling in front of the planter, he moved it a few inches. "How's that?"

"An inch more."

He complied. "Now?"

"Perfect."

Jake leaned back, resting his hands on his thighs. "This was a good idea. They really do brighten up the yard."

Sunni smiled, her expression peaceful.

" 'The desert and the parched land will be glad; the wilderness will rejoice and blossom.' "

Jake looked up at her. "Psalms?"

"Isaiah thirty-five. I was reading it this morning in the Bible Lynda gave me."

He scanned the yard. "Guess it's a little like a desert, but I wouldn't call it a wilderness."

Sunni laughed, brushing some dirt from her hands. "Neither would I, but it was a little bare. I think if your yard could talk, it would tell you that it's glad we've added some beauty to it."

Jake stood, too, unable to hold back a soft groan. Kneeling bothered him, but he'd rather deal with the pain he was used to than risk straining his back.

"What? Am I getting too corny for you?" She picked up the hose and turned on the faucet to water the plants.

"Nope. My leg just complains when I kneel or squat."

"Old football injury? I noticed in your high school annuals that you played running back on the varsity team." She moved to the next planter.

Jake laughed and stepped out of her way. "You really have been bored."

"I thought it might prompt some memories of my own school days."

"Did it?"

"No, but it was fun looking at the pictures." She watered the last batch of flowers. "And reading the notes people wrote. You were very popular, especially with the girls."

Jake leaned on the hand truck. "They liked everybody on the football team."

"Coyote Springs Coyotes. I don't suppose your sports teams could be called anything else."

"Nope. We were known far and wide for our stealth and cunning." His eyes twinkled and crinkled at the edges. "We called ourselves the Wily Coyotes."

Laughing, Sunni turned off the faucet and coiled up the hose. "Like the cartoon? I watched it for a few minutes this morning."

"Beep, beep." Jake grinned. "Only we spelled *wily* the regular way, so people got the right message. Sort of."

Sunni straightened and walked over to him. "So how did you hurt your leg?"

He considered letting her think it was a football injury. He had banged up his knee a couple of times. Only it was the other leg. He wouldn't lie, but he wouldn't elaborate on it, either. "Got shot while I was a Ranger." Her shocked expression made him

101

wish he'd stuck with the football story. "It's no big deal." Now.

"Yes, it is." Her brow creased into a worried frown. "Why didn't you tell me moving that pot again would make you hurt?"

"Because I didn't think about it." He started to brush away her frown with his fingertips but noticed they were dirty. He wiped them on his jeans instead. "I was having too much fun teasing you. My leg is already better and will be fine. I just need to walk a little and limber it up."

"I still wish you'd said something." She touched a plant on which the buds were only beginning to appear. "I hope I'm here when these bloom." The wistfulness in her voice surprised him.

"I hope so, too," he said quietly. He wanted it more than he cared to admit. "But I hope you have your memory back by then."

"What if it doesn't come back, Jake?"

"It will."

She looked up at him, a hint of fear hovering in her eyes again. "I don't know which would be worse — having a family waiting for me and thinking I've abandoned them or having no one, not mattering to anyone."

He put his arms around her, holding her close. "You aren't alone, Sunni. You have

102

people right here who care about you." He closed his eyes, resting his jaw against her hair. "I care about you." Much more than he should.

She slid her arms around his middle, hanging on tight. "I don't know what I'd do without you."

He held her a minute longer, then released her and eased from her embrace. "You'd find your way, Sunni. You're a survivor. Go on inside and rest. I'll put the hand truck away and be right in."

Megan's eight-year-old son, Drew, smacked the softball, sending it racing across the ground right toward second base. His six-year-old brother, Cody, had had a run a few minutes earlier that put him on first. The instant Drew hit the ball, Cody took off as fast as his little legs could carry him.

Jake was playing first baseman and Sunni third. Nobody was covering second. Sunni and Jake both raced toward the ball, then pulled up so they wouldn't crash into each other. Jake grabbed Sunni by the upper arms to steady her as the ball rolled right between them.

"Keep goin', guys," called Caleb, who was playing catcher. "Jake and Sunni think we're playing dodgeball."

Drew and Cody ran around the bases for all they were worth, urged on by Megan and Caleb's cheers. Drew had to slow up a little so he wouldn't go past his little brother. Jake trotted after the ball, stopping to look around for it.

Sunni wondered if he'd really lost it in the tall grass or if he was giving the boys a chance to score. When he spotted the ball and fumbled picking it up, she figured it was the latter. She glanced over her shoulder to see Drew heading for home. Cody had already touched the base and collapsed in the dirt out of the way. She held up her hand, waving the glove. "Here, Jake. You'll never make the throw to home."

He could, of course. He wasn't that far beyond the bases. Grinning, he carefully lobbed the ball to her. She caught it easily but she waited, giving Drew a little more time, before she winged it to Caleb, her throw straight and fast. The ball reached his mitt seconds after Drew crossed the plate.

Sunni froze. *The runner raced toward home, her expression hard and determined. The crowd's roar thundered in Sunni's ears as she focused on the catcher and let the ball fly, willing it to be the hardest, fastest, straightest throw she'd ever made. The ball reached the catcher's mitt seconds before the runner crossed the plate. Jubilation erupted in the stands on one side of the field as her team-mates surrounded her, laughing, shouting and jumping for joy. She searched the stands until she found a blond young man, his hands in the air, shaking his arms and screaming with the rest of them, beaming with pride because of her.*

"That was some throw." Jake jogged up beside her.

She clung to the memory and tried to take it farther, desperate to learn who *he* was, but it faded behind a cloud of mist.

Jake rested his hand on her shoulder. "Are you all right?"

Dazed, she looked up and brushed a strand of hair out of her eyes. Her hand shook, and he noticed.

"You need to sit down." He put his arm around her waist, ready to propel her toward the house.

"Wait," she said softly. "End the game however you can but give me a minute."

His arm tightened minutely as he called to Megan, "We're ready for cake and ice cream."

Megan laughed. "Coming right up." She started toward the house, and Caleb sent Jake a questioning look. When Jake nodded, his friend herded the boys after their mother. "Come on, kids, it's time for a victory celebration."

"Do we get extra ice cream because we won, Uncle Caleb?" begged Drew with a winsome smile.

"Maybe a little bit. What kind do you want?"

"Strawberry," shouted Cody, bouncing up and down as he walked.

"Vanilla." Drew chimed in only a little quieter than his brother.

Jake turned his attention back to Sunni. "You've played before, haven't you?"

"Yes. Maybe college. He was too old to be in high school. We all were."

"He?" Jake's heart lurched.

"A young man in the stands. Blond, attractive and so proud when I fired a ball to home and threw out the runner to win the game."

"Your boyfriend?" Or husband? He couldn't bring himself to say the word out loud.

"I don't know. I don't know who he was." She took a deep breath and met Jake's gaze. "But he loved me." Her eyes glistened with unshed tears. "Sometime, somewhere, someone loved me."

"Aw, Sunni." He pulled her into his arms for the second time that day. If he wasn't careful, it could become a habit. He closed his eyes, wishing for things that might never be. "Of course, you've been loved." Might still be. "You've probably had dozens of boyfriends, guys fightin' over you from the first day of kindergarten all the way through college. Black eyes, bloody noses, busted lips . . ."

She drew back, the tremulous beginning of a smile at odds with the trickle of tears rolling down her cheeks.

It about broke his heart.

Her smile won out. She wiped the tears with the heel of her hand and grinned. "What a way to make a woman feel better."

"Doin' my best, darlin'."

She looped her arm through his and turned toward the house. "Your best is pretty good, cowboy."

Half an hour later, after they finished off the bowls of chocolate cake and ice cream, Cody climbed up in Jake's lap and Drew plopped down beside him on the couch. "Tell us a story, Uncle Jake," said Cody.

"Yeah, one about catching a bad guy, with a car chase and lots of guns and shootin' and stuff." Drew held out his hand, pointing his index finger as if it were a pistol. "Pow! Pow! K-ching!"

Jake winced, and Sunni drew a sharp

breath at the pain flashing across his face. He hid it quickly, looking down at Drew with no hint of displeasure. "You boys have been watching too much television."

"Not so much," said Caleb with a shrug. "We played cops and robbers when we were kids."

"True." Jake shifted Cody on his lap. "It was different then. Robberies weren't so commonplace or so violent." He put one arm around Drew "Let's settle for a car chase."

"Okay." Both squirmed a little in their excitement.

"I was on patrol south of here on the road to San Angelo. Things had been quiet, everybody behaving themselves. I drove almost to Angelo and turned around and headed back this way. I needed a break from driving, so I parked all nice and sneaky behind an overpass where I could watch for speeders —"

"Boo!" interrupted Caleb with a grin. "Not fair!"

Jake ignored him. "A bright red Corvette flew by. Just a blur. I took off after that car in a second, lights flashing, siren wailing."

"How fast did you go?" Cody craned his neck around to look at him, his eyes wide.

"I hit eighty before I was close enough to

even see him again. Then ninety . . . ninety-five . . ."

Cody and Drew's eyes were as big as saucers.

"A hundred . . . a hundred ten . . . a hundred fifteen . . . and he was pulling away from me."

The boys' mouths fell open. Sunni snapped hers shut before Jake glanced her way.

"We were out there with no traffic and on a nice straight stretch, but I was worried that someone might pull out onto the road and never see him coming. Then that Corvette hit a little bump and he was airborne."

"Oh my!" Sunni's face grew warm at her outburst, but Jake just grinned. "Did he crash?"

"Nope. He touched back down on the road about thirty feet later with a little squeak of the tires, like a plane landing on an airstrip. But it made his hair stand on end — and he was wearin' a toupee."

Everybody but Cody laughed. Given the boy's puzzled expression, Sunni wondered if he knew what a toupee was. He tugged on Jake's shirtfront and leaned up, whispering in Jake's ear when he bent his head down. Jake whispered back and the little boy laughed.

He really loves these children, thought Sunni. He's so good with them. A bittersweet longing tugged at her heart. *Lord, do I have a dear little boy like Cody? Does he have a good man like Jake for his father? Is that why my heart aches?* Was some part of her subconscious trying to tell her that she had a husband and children? She was beginning to think not. Or if she did, perhaps she wasn't part of the family anymore. The thought was so depressing that she refused to dwell on it.

But it didn't stop the longing that someday she would have a husband and children to love and cherish.

"Did he give you any trouble?" asked Drew hopefully.

Sunni almost laughed out loud. The kid was still wanting some shoot-'em-up action. Jake met her gaze, a tiny smile lifting the corners of his mouth.

"No, he was very polite and cooperative. And shakin' like a leaf. Turned out he was a local politician. The car wasn't even his. He returned the car to his brother-in-law in San Angelo, paid his fine without a peep of protest, and word never got out about it. Except for the occasional tale like this where no names are mentioned."

"Which is almost as much of a miracle as

him not getting killed." Megan pointed her finger at Jake. "Or you, either."

"When we hit one hundred fifteen, I backed off." He glanced down at the youngsters. Cody's mouth stretched in a yawn and Drew was trying to stifle one. "Too dangerous for me. I'd gone faster than that before so I knew I could control the car, but then I'd been on a racetrack. Makes a big difference."

"Enough fun for today." Caleb pointed toward the hallway. "Time to get ready for bed, champs."

"Yes, sir. 'Night, Uncle Jake." Both boys gave him a quick hug. Drew smiled at Sunni and bade her good night, too. "I hope you can come back and play some more ball. You can be on our team next time."

"I'll plan on it. Thanks." Sunni smiled and told him good night.

Then Cody surprised her by giving her a hug, his little arms wrapped tightly around her neck. For a minute, she couldn't speak.

" 'Night, Miss Sunni."

"Good night, Cody. I'll ask Jake to bring me over again soon." She hugged him back.

When she released him, he nodded his head vigorously. "He will. He likes you a lot. You can talk him into doin' just about anything." The little boy grinned and raced down the hall.

Sunni glanced at Jake. Was the man actually blushing? He looked at her for a heartbeat then turned away, saying something to Caleb about his cows.

She helped Megan pick up the dessert bowls and carried them into the kitchen. Sunni rinsed them off and put them in the dishwasher while Megan covered the cake and put it away.

"Cody is right, you know." Megan leaned against the kitchen counter, speaking quietly. "Jake does like you a lot." Her voice held a subtle warning.

Sunni dried her hands on the towel lying on the counter. "But he's a wounded hero." She noted the surprise that flickered across Megan's face. "He hasn't said much about any heartache, except about his parents, but I've picked up a few things."

"Their deaths hurt him deeply."

"But something else happened, didn't it?" Sunni turned and wiped off the counter with the dishrag. "His leg bothered him this afternoon after we worked in the yard. He said he'd been shot while he was with the Texas Rangers, but that it wasn't a big deal. How can being shot not be a big deal?"

"It was awful. He took two bullets. The one that hit his leg broke the thigh bone just above the knee. He has a rod and pins holding it together."

Grimacing, Sunni draped the cloth over the edge of the dish drainer. "Now, I really feel bad about him working so hard today."

"You shouldn't. He often works hard, and he was fine by the time we played ball. He doesn't let it slow him down. He spent months in physical therapy, so I guess he learned what to do if it bothers him. The injury that had us on our knees for days was the chest wound."

Like the man in my dream. Sunni gasped softly, turning her back toward the living room in case Jake glanced her way. He would instantly know something was wrong, and if he didn't come check on her, he'd ask about it on the way home. She'd had the dream again three nights earlier. She still hadn't seen the man's face, but there had been blood all over his chest. When she awakened, her heartache had been even deeper than before.

Just thinking about Jake being hurt in a similar way brought tears to her eyes.

"Sunni, are you okay?" Megan asked quietly.

"Yes." She blinked back the tears and picked a dead leaf off a potted plant in the windowsill to try to mask her reaction. "Just thinking about Jake being so seriously hurt . . ."

"I know. Almost every time I see him, I praise the Lord for sparing him." Megan fussed with another plant in the window, keeping her back to the living room, too.

"The bullet broke a couple of ribs. One of them punctured his lung. The lung collapsed and air escaped into the space between his lung and the chest wall. He had two operations, one on his chest and one on his leg, in a matter of hours. He was in ICU for several days with a tube in his chest to suction the air out. He'd lost tons of blood and had to have a transfusion."

"Was there any permanent damage?"

"Not physically. Miraculously, the bullet missed his organs. The surgeons took care of the lung and damaged muscles, and the ribs eventually healed. But another officer was killed during the gun battle. Jake has never gotten over that."

"Is that why he quit the Rangers?"

"I think the whole thing just got to him. You saw the way he flinched when Drew was pretending to shoot a pistol."

"Jake was wearing a gun when he found me."

"In case he tangled with a rattler or some other angry critter. We've had a few outbreaks of rabies in the wild animals over the years, so it pays to be prepared. That's a whole lot different than facing someone who's firing back."

"He seems to enjoy ranching."

"He does, but he's lonely. Not that he'd ever admit it." Megan put soap in the dishwasher and turned it on. "Having you around is good for him, keeps him from dwelling on the past. Looking after you has given him a reason to care about life again. And there lies the dilemma."

"What will happen when my memory returns."

"Exactly."

"I'll do everything I can to keep from hurting him."

"I know you will. I hope it's enough."

CHAPTER SIX

The next morning, Sunni put on a pretty lavender embroidered blouse, a pair of jeans and sandals. She went in search of Lynda, finding her in the kitchen. "I think I'm ready to go. Are you sure I'm dressed okay for church? I watched a service last week on TV and the people were really dressed up."

"That was the big city." Lynda waved her hand, making the multicolored bangles on her wrist tinkle. "Or some folks in Coyote Springs. Out here in the country, just about everyone opts for comfort. Showing up is what counts."

"You're not wearing jeans." Sunni admired Lynda's pretty crinkled cotton outfit. The bright coral should have clashed with her red hair, but it didn't.

"No, but this still falls in the casual category. Toby said he might attend this morning, so I spiffed up a bit."

"So, are you two an item?"

Lynda laughed. "I wouldn't say that. I like him, though. And I think he likes me."

Jake strolled down the hall from his office. "Of course he likes you. Everybody likes you." He gave his aunt a mischievous grin. "But Toby likes you more than most."

A little blush warmed Lynda's cheeks. "I hope you're not just saying that to make me feel good, rascal."

"I'm not. Toby has been going to church as long as I've known him, but I think it would take more than Ron's preaching to get him to drive all the way out here on Sunday morning." He tipped his head up and sniffed. "Though that pot roast you're cooking might have something to do with it."

"Don't forget to put the vegetables in around eleven. They're all cut up."

"Yes, ma'am." He turned to Sunni, his gaze skimming over her before settling on her face. "Both you ladies look very nice this morning."

"Thanks." She almost told him that he looked pretty good himself. Maybe a little too comfortable in his everyday turquoise Western shirt and well-worn jeans for even a casual church service, but just fine for her. She figured he'd look great no matter what, which presented her with a dilemma of her own.

Their situation was unique, and being attracted to him was probably natural but not necessarily wise. No matter how much her mind told her to keep up her guard, her lonely heart didn't seem to pay any heed to the admonitions.

"I need to get my Bible." Mindful of Jake's uncanny knack for sensing her moods and reading her expressions, she made her escape down the hall. She took a few minutes to rein in her wayward thoughts, then picked up the Bible and small straw purse Lynda had given her.

As she walked back toward the kitchen, she heard Jake talking to his aunt. The intensity of his quiet voice prompted her to stop in the hallway and look at the family pictures there. Though she didn't do it to eavesdrop, she couldn't help overhearing their conversation.

"Stick close to her and if anybody starts giving her a bad time, shut it down." The thread of steel in Jake's tone made Sunni blink.

"There won't be a problem, hon. They're good people, compassionate and understanding."

"Even church people gossip sometimes,"

he said sarcastically.

"The only person who might be the least bit catty is Nadine Sherlock, but she's visiting her sister in Missouri for a couple of months."

"If she's there —"

"Jake, don't worry. She won't be."

"What if —"

"If she came home early, I'll keep her away from Sunni. But she won't, not with her sister lining her up with blind dates every few nights."

"Hope it works and she stays in Missouri."

Lynda laughed. "Tired of dodging her?"

"Wore out a pair of boots running the other way."

Sunni decided it was safe to go on into the kitchen. "I didn't figure you'd run from anything."

"Just a very stubborn bell chaser."

"As in wedding bells." Lynda grinned and picked up her purse and Bible from the counter. "One of the rancher's daughters has her eye on our sweet Jake. She's only nineteen."

"And acts about fifteen. She was calling me every half hour. I had to get caller ID."

"That's why you always check it before you answer the phone," said Sunni, trying not to laugh.

He shrugged and leaned back against the counter. "Better to ignore her than hang up on her. How long has she been gone?"

"A couple of weeks."

"She hasn't called for three." His face brightened. "Hey, maybe she's given up."

"One would hope that after a year she's gotten the message." Lynda glanced at the two of them, appeared to almost say something, then decide against it. "We'd better hit the road, Sunni. Don't want to be late."

"And make Toby think you've stood him up." Jake wiggled his eyebrows.

"Can't have that." Lynda went out the back door, letting the screen door slam behind her.

Jake caught Sunni's arm in a gentle grip and handed her his cell phone. "If anybody says one word that hurts or offends you, just walk away. Call me and I'll come get you. The number is programmed in under *home*."

Poor Jake, who hurt you so badly? "I'm sure it will be fine. But I'll take this if it will make you feel better." She slipped the phone into her purse. "I've looked forward to going to church and worshipping with other believers all week. Someone would have to be awfully hateful to make me leave."

120

He stared at the floor and sighed. "Your expectations are probably more accurate than mine. Most folks there are good people."

"But it only takes one to twist a knife," she said softly.

"Yeah." He looked up. The pain in his eyes was almost enough to make her stay home.

Home? This place was the only home she had. For now. All that could change in an instant.

"I'm tough. A survivor, remember?" She reached up, lightly cupping his jaw. He moved a fraction, pressing his face against her hand. "Besides, God is with me. How can anyone be against me?"

"You're wearin' the full armor, that's a fact." A hint of sadness lingered in his face when she slowly lowered her hand. "You'd better scoot before Lynda starts honking the horn and scares Licorice. He'll carry on something fierce."

Sunni mustered a smile when what she really wanted to do was take him in her arms and comfort him the way he had done her so many times. "How about a tour of the ranch this afternoon?"

"Sounds good." The sadness vanished, and he followed her toward the door. "It'll give Toby and Lynda a chance to be alone."

And us, too. For a second, she thought she might have actually whispered the words, but when she glanced over her shoulder, his expression hadn't changed. Then he looked into her eyes, and her heart did a flip-flop. If she hadn't said it, he was thinking the same thing. "See you later."

He nodded. As she went out the screen door, she thought she heard him say softly, "Enjoy."

Jake tried to do some bookkeeping after they left, but he couldn't concentrate. He kept worrying about somebody being unkind to Sunni, then told himself that he was being silly. There was no reason for anybody to say anything to her. She hadn't done anything wrong.

Not that we know about anyway. He picked up a tennis ball from his desk and threw it against the wall, catching it when it flew back toward him. He threw it again, so hard it made a mark on the wall — one of many — and stung his hand when he caught it. He didn't for a second believe she was involved in anything criminal, immoral or even unethical.

"Then why do I do that? Why do I always have to analyze things, look for ulterior motives or the possibility of wrongdoing? Why can't I quit thinking like a cop?" He dropped the ball, letting it bounce across the floor. Licorice scrambled after it, proudly trotting off down the hall, carrying his prize.

Jake spun around and rested his elbows on his desk. Leaning his forehead on his hands, he ran his fingers through his hair and closed his eyes. "She's too fine and decent a person to do anything wrong. Probably has never even jaywalked. So there's no reason for anyone to treat her badly."

Unlike him. He'd caused the death of a fine officer and friend. More than a friend. Only a few people in Austin, plus Caleb and probably Megan, knew that he and Pam had been romantically involved for six months when she died. They hadn't talked about marriage, but he'd thought things were headed that way.

If they'd hardly known each other, if he didn't remember her smile, her laughter, her touch . . . Maybe then it would be easier to forgive himself. Easier to think God might forgive him for drifting away from Him long before that tragic day. If he'd been living right and walking closer, maybe God never would have let it happen.

He straightened with a heavy sigh. "Wishing things had been different won't change a thing." He didn't deserve forgiveness, and he didn't have the right to forget. Or to fall at the feet of Jesus and be made whole again.

Jake went into the kitchen and put the vegetables in the pot, turning up the heat for a few minutes until the liquid started bubbling again. He turned the heat back down to low and checked the time. Had they really only been gone thirty minutes? It seemed as if they had left hours ago.

How could he miss her so much in such a short time? He practically snorted. Licorice looked up from where he was napping in the hall and tipped his head to the side, his ears perking up.

"I miss her the same way I have all week whenever I left the house. Only it's worse after we spent the day together yesterday."

Licorice got up and walked into the kitchen, sitting at Jake's feet. Jake could have sworn the dog frowned and looked at him with great concern. He leaned down and patted his furry friend on the head. "I've got it bad, Lic, and I don't know what to do about it."

Licorice smiled his winsome doggy grin, wagged his tail and looked over at his jar of treats.

Jake laughed and tossed the dog a bone-shaped biscuit. "Reckon you deserve that for lifting my spirits. Let me set the table and then we'll go outside and play for a while."

Maybe that would make the time go faster.

The church service was all Sunni had hoped it would be. To her joy, she discovered that she recognized most of the songs and even knew some of them by heart. The people were warm and welcoming when they took a friendship break after the singing. There was some curiosity, but mainly people seemed concerned about her well-being.

Lynda, Toby and Sunni were talking to some of Jake's neighbors, Ralph and Irene, when the minister approached. They wished her well and stepped aside so he could talk to her.

"Is this our miracle lady?" he asked with a delightful smile.

"It is." Lynda put her arm around Sunni's shoulders in a hug. "Sunni, this is Pastor Ron Armstrong."

"Just call me Ron. Everybody does. Welcome to Kincaid Community."

"Thanks. It's nice to meet you. The singing has been lovely, a real blessing."

"I hope the sermon will be a blessing, too, and not put you to sleep. We're glad to have you with us, Sunni." His expression sobered. "Has your memory returned? Or do we need to keep praying about that?"

"Keep praying, please." Lynda had told her that she'd put the request on the church's prayer line, but having the minister ask about it made her realize that they really had been holding her — a complete stranger — up before God's throne. "I've remembered a few things, but nothing that tells me much about myself."

He shook his head. "I've tried to imagine what that would be like, but it's impossible. Lynda tells me that you love the Lord. It's pretty obvious that He loves you. I believe God is going to use this whole experience in a good way for you and those around you."

"All things for His purpose," murmured Toby.

"Exactly. I certainly don't know what it is," said Ron, "but He does."

"That's what I'm counting on." Sunni moved over a step as a couple of little kids went racing by.

"Well, I'll quit monopolizing you. Other people want to meet you." He started to turn away but stopped and looked back at her. "Tell Jake to come see me. I miss him. We all do."

Sunni swallowed the thickness that formed in her throat. Several others had made similar comments. They cared for Jake. What kept him away? "I'll tell him."

"Good. Maybe you can get him to come back. So far Lynda and I haven't had any success."

She met several more people, though she had forgotten half their names by the time she sat back down. The sermon was interesting, but Sunni's mind kept drifting, her thoughts on Jake. He should have been there. He needed to be there, to be loved, to be blessed and uplifted by the worship songs and the pastor's message. *Father God, be with Jake right this minute. Draw him to You, Lord. Somehow, let him know how much You love him. Heal his hurt, his sorrow, whatever keeps him away from You.*

She focused again on what Pastor Ron was saying only to realize that he was winding up the service.

On the way home, she asked Lynda about Jake. "Why doesn't he go to church anymore?"

Lynda slowed down, turned and drove through the cattle guard. When she didn't answer, Sunni decided she'd made a mistake. "I'm sorry, I'm out of line asking that."

"No, it's okay. I'm just not sure how to answer. I doubt if I know the whole of it. The situation is complicated, and one I think Jake should explain to you. If he will." She glanced at Sunni. "I don't think he's talked about it much to anyone, but he might open up to you. While he was with the Texas Rangers, he was seriously injured in a shooting."

"He told me he'd been shot in the leg but brushed it off as insignificant. Last night Megan told me about all his injuries and that the other officer was killed."

"It happened in Austin. Jake had transferred there from the Midland office about ten months earlier. There was an investigation, of course, and lots of speculation, especially on the part of the press, that Jake was responsible for the deputy's death, that he froze. Some people in her department called him a coward, and it was picked up by the newspapers and radio talk shows.

"Two or three families in town have relatives in Austin, so they kept them up-to-date on all the news, good and bad, which provided fodder for the local gossip mill. Some folks simply have to tear others down to build themselves up. Unfortunately, a couple who occasionally went to Kincaid Community at the time were some of the worst at dragging people through the mud.

"They quit attending there after Pastor Ron took them to task for it, but Jake still refused to go to church. When he went to town, some people whispered about him. It was painfully obvious what they were doing. A couple of the good ol' boys called him a coward behind his back. He heard about it but didn't do anything. He figured it would be the same at church, though he should have known better. But when a man's heart and soul are trampled as badly as his, he builds high walls in self-defense."

"Maybe I shouldn't mention it to him. I don't want to open up old wounds."

"That wound won't heal until he deals with his grief and guilt. He blames himself for the deputy's death. I don't know why but he does. The investigation cleared him, but Jake can't let it go. Maybe you're the one who can help him do that." She parked the car behind the house and turned off the ignition.

Toby stopped his patrol car beside them as Jake came out the back door and headed toward Sunni's side of the car. *Lord, give me the right words at the right time.* Jake opened her door, his frown easing when she gave him a bright smile.

"How was it?" He opened the door wider so she could get out of the car.

She noted that Toby was doing the same for Lynda. "Good. I actually knew some of the songs and recognized the others."

"Which tells us you've gone to church more than a time or two."

"Being there felt right. The people were friendly, maybe a little curious but not obnoxious about it. Several said to give you their best. Pastor Ron said he missed you."

"That's what he tells me when he calls every other week." He fell in step beside her as they walked to the house.

"So, unlike Nadine's calls, you answer his."

"Don't know why. They're both trying to reel me in."

"But he has good motives."

"Such as?"

"It's better to be safe in the boat than adrift at sea."

"Hear that in the sermon this morning?"

"Nope. Thought it up all by myself." She gave him a sassy grin.

And was rewarded with a hint of a smile.

CHAPTER SEVEN

Toby set his fork on the empty dessert plate and leaned back with a groan. "Delicious dinner, Lynda."

"Yes, it was." Sunni scooted the chair back and began clearing the table. "I'm stuffed. If I don't stand up now, I won't be able to move for an hour."

"Need a wheelbarrow to haul me away," chimed in Jake, contradicting his statement by standing and stacking up some dishes. "You outdid yourself on that apple pie. I don't think you've ever made one better."

"Thanks for the compliments." Lynda laid her napkin on the table and relaxed with a grin. "Everything did turn out pretty good."

"Perfect." Toby winked at Lynda and drank the last sip of his coffee.

Sunni glanced at Jake, noting that he watched the exchange between his aunt and old friend with a hint of amusement. She might smack him with the dish towel if he teased them. "Why don't y'all go find a comfy place to relax while Jake and I do the dishes?"

His attention snapped to her, followed by a wide grin.

"What did I say?"

"Y'all."

Sunni set the stack of dessert plates down on the table with a clunk. "I did?"

"Yep. And obviously you didn't even notice. Told you that you'd pick up the lingo before you knew it."

"Well, if that don't beat all." Sunni picked up the dishes and headed for the kitchen.

Laughing, Jake was right behind her, carrying the roast platter and a bowl with the few remaining potatoes and carrots. "Where did you pick that up?"

"Rita Mae must have said it half-a-dozen times while I was in the hospital."

"While you were relating your story, no doubt." He set the platter and bowl on the counter and retrieved some plastic containers from a drawer.

"Yes." Sunni rinsed a plate and stuck it in the dishwasher. A strand of hair tickled her cheek, and she tried to push it back with her shoulder. "She was duly amazed."

"She should be." He brushed her hair back, tucking it behind her ear. "You're an amazing woman."

His soft voice and the tenderness of his touch made her knees go weak. *Oh, my.* She gripped the edge of the sink, closing her eyes.

He put his arm around her. "Did you have another memory?"

Shaking her head, she looked up at him and took a deep, steadying breath. "No. Just making a new one."

His eyes darkened, and his fingers flexed against her side. "Hurry up with those dishes, so we can get out of here." Releasing her, he dumped the vegetables and roast into the containers and snapped on the lids.

He brought in the rest of the dishes, and she rinsed them off. Holding a bowl down for Licorice, he let the dog finish off the last of the green beans. "There you go, boy, that's your dessert."

They were done cleaning up the kitchen in less than ten minutes. Jake glanced at the clock and chuckled. "Think we set a new record."

"No sense dawdling when there's a ranch to see."

"Then let's hightail it." He stopped and looked at her feet. "You'd better change into your other shoes. If we decide to walk around, those sandals won't cut it."

"Be right back." Sunni took a few extra minutes. As it was, Toby and Lynda would probably have a good laugh about how quick she and Jake ran off to be by themselves. Or ran off to leave the older couple alone. She hoped they would think the latter. When she walked into the living room, Jake was telling them about their plans.

"I promised Sunni that I'd drive her around the ranch for a while this afternoon. She hasn't had a chance to see much. Since it's a little cooler this afternoon —"

"Cooled all the way down to eighty," Toby said dryly. "Havin' a cold spell."

"Better make sure the cows aren't gettin' frostbite." Jake looked up at Sunni. "Ready?"

"Should we grab some bottles of water?"

"Definitely. I'll get some for Lic, too."

"Don't tell me he drinks out of a bottle."

"No, just the hose. I keep a water dish behind the back seat of the truck."

Within a few minutes they were settled in the truck and on their way, not bothering with the seat belts since they wouldn't be on any public roads or running into traffic. They drove down a hill and across the valley, past some cattle resting in the shade of a small grove of mesquites. Small patches of yellow and purple wildflowers mingled with the grass.

"We'll check the tank and see how the water is holding up." Jake veered off the dirt road, bouncing through the pasture, dodging the occasional mesquite or prickly pear. Soon a big dirt hole with sloping sides came into view. It was more than half full of water.

"That looks like a pond. Isn't a tank some kind of container?"

"It's containing the water." He smiled that lazy smile of his, the one that made her feel a little wobbly inside. "I suppose in some places it would be considered a pond. Probably made the same way, with a bulldozer. Though I don't recall ever seeing any ducks swimming around on it."

A cow wandered down a trail through the grass and into the tank, stopping a few feet into the water, and lowered her head for a drink.

"It certainly seems to serve the purpose."

"Unless we have a drought. Then it gets a little tricky. Our normal average rainfall is a little over nineteen inches a year. If we don't get that much, which we often don't, we have problems. We caught about a foot of water from the last rain. The tank is placed so it will get the runoff from a couple of draws." At her puzzled frown, he pointed to one end of it. "A draw is a gully or a creek bed that's normally dry."

"I walked through a bunch of those. Though they didn't look like creek beds."

"Most weren't. There are two actual creeks running through the ranch. The one you were following, Fraser Creek, has water in it all year because it originates from a spring."

"Which came first, naming the creek or the ranch?"

"The creek, because Grandpa Colin was just camped there for a while by the spring. As soon as he bought some of the land, he dubbed it a ranch. The other, Muddy Creek, hasn't had water in it for years. We're fighting a battle to preserve the aquifer underneath this whole section of the country.

"I had the brush cleared out from Muddy Creek this last winter. There were a lot of salt cedars growing there. If any water trickled down the creek when it rained, they took it. I don't know how much good it will do overall, or if I'll ever see the creek flowing again. But at least when we get rain, it will soak into the ground and eventually the aquifer instead of the unbeneficial salt cedars using it."

Jake put the pickup in gear and made a wide turn, going back to the road. They went over another cattle guard in the barbed wire fence. She couldn't see any difference in the pastures.

"Why is there a fence here? It looks the same on both sides."

"It is. The ranch used to be divided into four big pastures, but my dad split it up into twelve. It's easier to round up the cattle in smaller ones. Some are still a good size, difficult for one man to gather all the cows by himself. It also makes it easier to control the grazing. When the grass gets low in one, we move them to another."

"We?"

"Caleb usually helps me. Or one of his men if he can't do it. He's coming over tomorrow to help me move part of the herd to the pasture where I found you."

"The grass was still fairly long and green there."

"That's right. We're gonna make a rancher out of you yet."

Sunni laughed. "I think there's a whole lot more to ranching than knowing that tall, green grass will make fat cows."

"True. But it's a good start."

Sunni pointed to a surprisingly large area where the mesquites had all been cut down. "Did you decide to heat the house with your fireplace last winter?"

"I used some of it for that, probably have

about a five-year supply. A guy in town went into the mesquite charcoal business, so I offered him as much free wood as he wanted as long as he cut it and hauled it away. Saved me the work and expense of trying to clear it.

"This area in particular was overgrazed years ago, so the mesquites were thick. They have an extensive root system and use a lot of water, to the detriment of the grass. Sometimes ranchers bulldoze them or hook a big chain between a couple of bulldozers and drag them up. Some burn them out or spray them with herbicide. Nothing seems to keep them down permanently. And there are downsides to all the methods.

"I'm fortunate that my ancestors didn't overgraze the land all over the ranch the way it was in this section. So most of it hasn't been overrun with mesquites. Having some are good since they provide shade for the cows and homes for birds and other wild critters. But it's a fine balancing act. One I'm not sure I've figured out yet."

"If your friend keeps needing wood, won't that help?"

"It will if he can make a go of it. He works for the telephone company so it's a side enterprise now."

A few minutes later, he turned down

another road, going south. "We'll check the windmill while we're over here. It's by an old house with several big chinaberry trees in the yard. It's a nice place to sit and rest in the shade for a spell."

"I didn't think you ever rested. You always seem to be doing something."

"I like to keep busy." So he wouldn't think about troublesome things. The past. The future. Her. They all seemed intertwined, and no matter how hard he worked, none of them were far from his thoughts. Especially her. "But I take a break occasionally. Like now."

"But you're still working, checking on the windmill."

"Just being practical. It saves me another trip over here." He drove around another stand of mesquites and pointed to the windmill and old house, resting on a little hill. "I suppose I should tear it down, but I hate to. Grandpa and Grandma Trayner lived here in the early forties. It was a decent place then." He pulled up in the shade and shut off the engine.

"It isn't in terrible shape, just a little weather-beaten."

"Weather battered is more like it. I'm not sure it could be made habitable." Jake opened the door and climbed out of the truck, noting that Sunni did the same. He let Licorice out the back door. "Don't wander off, dog. We won't be here all afternoon."

Sunni came around the front of the pickup, watching as Licorice trotted off around the side of the house, nose to the ground. "Will he obey you?"

"No, but he's good about not going too far. He's caught the scent of something." The dog appeared again, sniffing the ground, going in a winding trail around the yard. "Probably a rabbit or a possum."

She walked across the yard, stopping in front of the house. Jake followed, surveying the valley and hills on the other side. The grass was still tall and green in the valley. Broad swaths of purple verbena covered the hilly slopes. There was also a mass of it near the house, filling the air with its sweet fragrance. "This is one of my favorite places on the ranch."

"I can see why. It's lovely. But I don't know if I'd want to live here. It seems awfully isolated."

"I don't think my grandparents minded. They were newlyweds and, according to my grandpa, her father would have run rough-shod over them if they'd been closer to the ranch house."

"Was she a Fraser?"

"Yes, and an only child. Grandpa was a cowboy who worked on the ranch."

"And married the boss's daughter. Smart man."

Jake laughed and took her hand. "Yeah, he was. Do you want to peek inside?"

"Sure."

They walked up on the creaky porch, and Jake opened the door, leaving it wide-open to allow in more light. He stepped inside first and scanned the room, then moved over so Sunni could join him. "I don't see any varmints but watch for snakes."

"Snakes?" She grabbed hold of his arm. "I don't think I like snakes."

"I know I don't. But they don't like us, either, so if any were here, they've probably already skedaddled." He pried her fingers loose and put his arm around her. "There's not a lot to see anyway. Just three rooms."

The tour took five minutes, if that.

When they were back in the living room, Sunni looked around with a frown. "There's no bathroom."

"Outhouse." He pointed out the back window. "If this place wasn't so well hidden, that outhouse would have disappeared long ago."

"Surely an antiques collector wouldn't

141

steal an outhouse."

"I wouldn't be surprised. But more often, it's high school kids wanting it to play a prank on somebody. Or to add to a homecoming bonfire. A couple were 'donated' to bonfires when I was in school. But I never mentioned this one. My dad had too many funny tales about it to see it go up in smoke."

"But where did they take a bath?"

They walked out onto the porch, and he pulled the door tightly closed. He didn't bother locking it. If anyone ever wanted in, they'd just go through one of the broken windows. "They used a washtub, one of those big round galvanized tubs. The same one Grandma washed their clothes in. But she was fortunate. Since they had the windmill, Grandpa piped running water into the kitchen, so they didn't have to carry the bucket very far."

He took her out back and showed her the windmill and large metal water trough for the cattle. "Good, everything's working fine. Climbing up top isn't my favorite job."

She tipped her head way back and looked up at the big wheel of the windmill. "You climb way up there?"

"Only when I have to. The view is really something from up there though."

"I'll take your word for it."

He thought she was going to say something more but stopped, a frown creasing her brow. "Do you remember something about falling down the cliff?"

"No. Never mind." She smiled up at him, but he could tell something was bothering her.

"Sunni, what is it?"

"Megan told me you had pins and a rod in your leg. Should you be climbing up there at all?"

"I can do anything I need to." Annoyed with Megan for spouting off and with Sunni for questioning his abilities, his tone was harsh. "What else did she tell you?"

Sunni stood her ground with quiet dignity. He had to admire her spunk.

"She said you were shot in the chest, had a collapsed lung and almost died. That another officer was killed, and that you had never gotten over it."

"That's it?"

"That's all she said." She glanced away.

If she'd been in a police interrogation, he would have been as suspicious as a goat eyeing a new gate. "But somebody else said more? Lynda?"

She looked every direction but at him.

Exasperated, Jake gritted his teeth and

counted to five. No way would he make it to ten. "What did my dear aunt, who of course meant no harm, have to say about my personal — and private — business?"

Sunni blew out a breath and shoved that often wayward strand of hair back out of her face. "This was not the way I meant to bring this up."

"You've opened the bag, you might as well let all the cats out."

"I need some water first. Then we can sit down in the shade and talk about this like calm, rational people."

"All right." Even if he didn't feel the least bit calm or rational. He needed a few minutes to cool off, though it wasn't the kind of cooldown sitting in the shade would accomplish. "I'll get the water."

He went to the truck for Licorice's dish and the small cooler with the water bottles. When he returned, Sunni was using a broken branch still full of leaves to brush aside the chinaberries that had fallen on the ground beneath the biggest tree. It had grown out the side of a stump probably thirty years earlier, so the base was actually wide enough for two people to have a back-rest.

"There, I think that cleared them out of the way. Dirt will wash out, but I don't want to squish anything on these new jeans." She sat down primly, taking the bottle he handed her and opening it.

Jake got some water, too, and sat down beside her — right beside her. Had she cleaned such a small space on purpose? He took a swig of water and waited until she had a long drink. "Okay, woman. Talk."

CHAPTER EIGHT

Jake stretched his legs out straight and waited for Sunni to begin. He could understand Megan blabbing about his injuries although she didn't have a gossipy bone in her body. She hadn't lived at the ranch as a kid, but she had visited often so they'd known each other practically all their lives. He'd been like another big brother to her.

He had caught her watching him and Sunni, no doubt noticing the attraction between them. He tried not to be obvious, but it was hard to hide his interest. Even Cody had noticed it. And in her typical gotta-protect-my-big-brother way, Megan would have tried to clue Sunni in about him.

"Don't be angry at them," Sunni said quietly. "Megan was concerned about you being hurt when my memory returns." She picked up a long twig and methodically snapped it into little pieces. "She was trying to let me know that you'd been hurt before.

I'd already sensed that. You hide it pretty well, but sometimes I see the pain in your eyes."

She turned away, picking up another twig, absently rolling it around between her fingers. "This morning I overheard you and Lynda talking before we left for church. I was coming down the hall after getting my Bible and purse."

Jake tensed, trying to remember exactly what he'd said to his aunt. He'd been talking about people gossiping, but how much had he revealed?

"I should have gone back to my room, but I didn't. I stayed there in the hall and listened. I'm sorry. It was wrong. Given your tone, it was apparent that you'd been hurt by gossip, maybe even from someone at church. Then when we were talking right before Lynda and I left, there was so much pain in your eyes that I almost stayed home."

Surprised, he focused on her face. She was looking out across the yard, still twisting that little twig in her hand. She'd called his place home.

"So when at least half-a-dozen people at church asked about you, it took me by surprise. They wished you well, or said they missed seeing you there. After we left, I asked Lynda why you didn't go to church anymore."

"And she bent your ear all the way home." Being talkative was his aunt's nature. Revealing personal things about someone else wasn't. Maybe he was jumping to conclusions.

"No." *Snap.* Another twig was destined to become tiny beauty bark. *Snap.* "She told me that there was a lot of speculation in Austin after the shooting, especially in the media, saying you were responsible for the other officer's death, that you froze. A few people even called you a coward." *Snap.* "Some people here heard all about the investigation from relatives in Austin. That kept the local gossip mill going at full blast, and some, including a couple who occasionally attended Kincaid Community, dragged your name in the mud."

Her hands stilled and she looked at him again. "I can't imagine anyone who claims to be a Christian being so mean."

"Claiming it doesn't necessarily mean they are. Even if someone believes in Jesus for their salvation, they don't always live the way they should." He knew that firsthand.

"I know. But I don't understand why you won't go back to Kincaid Community now. Those awful people aren't there anymore."

"What else did Lynda tell you?" He was relieved that his voice sounded almost normal.

"She said you blamed yourself for the death of the other officer, that the investigation cleared you, but you couldn't let it go."

"It was my fault." The fact was branded in his memory, along with every detail of that afternoon.

"The investigators said you weren't to blame."

"No, they didn't."

"What?" She stared at him, dropping the last tiny bit of the stick.

"They said they couldn't be certain that she would have lived even if I'd done things differently. They worded it carefully, fancied it up some, but they never actually cleared me. They couldn't." Bending his right knee, he rested his forearm on it and moved so he could look into her face. "The man had a gun, and I ordered him to put it down. I saw him raise it to fire, but I didn't shoot him. At least not quickly enough."

"Surely, you had a good reason not to."

"He was an embezzler named Henderson. It was supposed to be an easy arrest. When we knocked on the door of his condo, his nine-year-old daughter opened it and let us in." The scene played out in his mind as it had a thousand times. "I went in first, and Pam followed with her gun drawn. The kid didn't notice the gun. I asked the girl where her daddy was, and she said in the bedroom. She ran off to tell him we were there before I could stop her. So I drew my weapon, too. Pam did a quick check of the kitchen to make sure it was clear, then stepped back into the living room."

Shifting again, Jake rested his back and head against the tree. He didn't want to see her face as he repeated what he had told the investigators. And perhaps a few things more.

"Henderson came out of the bedroom, telling his daughter to stay there. He had a pistol and was waving it around erratically. I ordered him to drop the gun. He hollered at us to get out and leave them alone. I ordered him to drop the gun again, and he lowered it. I thought he was actually going to toss it on the floor. Then his hand slowly started back up, the pistol pointed right at me.

"There was a movement behind him, and his little girl stepped into the bedroom doorway. I glanced at her and shook my head. She just looked at me, those great big terrified brown eyes begging me not to shoot her daddy. It was only a few seconds, but that's all it took.

"Pam yelled at him to drop his weapon. He jerked the gun toward her and fired. She went down, but I couldn't get a clear shot because his daughter was trying to grab him, screaming at him to stop. Once he started shooting, he kept pulling the trigger. There was nothing to hide behind. All the furniture was on the other side of the room. Weird, ultramodern stuff that wouldn't have stopped a bullet anyway.

"I got hit in the leg and fell. He shoved his daughter away, and I fired. So did he. It was strange, like an old-time western movie. I saw my bullet hit him in the chest a heartbeat before his hit me.

"Somehow, I dragged myself over to Pam." He closed his eyes and drew a shuddering breath, the heartache almost more than he could bear. "I touched her hand, and she looked at me. I could see the bewilderment in her eyes. Not an accusation, just a question — why didn't you shoot? Then she drew her last breath, and I passed out. The neighbors called 911, otherwise I would have died there, too."

"Well, I'm very glad you didn't."

He forced himself to look at her and then wished he hadn't. Tears poured down her cheeks.

"And not just so you could save me." She embraced him, holding him fiercely, the top of her head tucked against his jaw. Her tears quickly dampened his shirt.

He put his arms around her, accepting her comfort, desperately wishing it truly could ease the agony in his heart. But it wasn't that simple. A gentle, compassionate woman couldn't assuage his sins, guilt and pain.

"Jake, lay your guilt on the altar, give it to God and receive His forgiveness. Let Him take it away so you can forgive yourself."

"I can't, Sunni. I don't deserve forgiveness — from God or from myself."

She eased back, straightening so she could look up at him, resting her hand on his chest. "None of us deserves God's forgiveness. It's a gift. The Bible says that if we confess our sins, He is faithful and just and will forgive us our sins and purify us from all unrighteousness."

"I have plenty that needs purifying." He moved away from her, pushing against the tree so he could get up. "Sunni, you don't understand. I don't have the right to ask God to ease my pain or forgive my sins. I walked away from Him a long time ago."

Surprise swept across her face, then something more. Disapproval? No, disappointment. He'd expected it, but it only added to his misery.

"Why?" she asked quietly as she stood.

"I'm not even sure how it happened. Working a lot of Sundays with the Highway Patrol, missing church, being in a different town so nobody at church noticed when I wasn't there." He flexed his fingers, wishing he'd picked up one of those little twigs, too. "After I joined the Rangers, my job pretty much became my whole life. It wasn't like one day I decided that I didn't need Him or love Him or want to live for Him. I just slowly grew to depend on myself, not God, in dangerous situations as well as everyday life.

"When I met Pam, I hadn't been to church in years. She was a deputy sheriff in Austin. A mutual friend introduced us at a law enforcement barbecue, and we hit it off right from the start."

Understanding dawned on her face. "She was more than just someone you were working with that day."

Jake nodded, hanging his head as the memories hit him again. "We'd worked a few cases together before, only because the higher-ups didn't know we were dating." Heaving a sigh, he forced himself to look at her. "We weren't just dating."

"Were you living together?"

"We each had our own apartment, but we might as well have shared one." He turned away from her perceptive gaze. "I knew what we were doing was wrong, a sin in God's eyes. But I was so far away from Him that I didn't let it bother me. Not enough to change, anyway."

"Did you love her?"

"I thought I was falling in love with her. I cared for her, but I hadn't reached the point where I wanted to commit to marriage, to a lifetime together." He rubbed the tense muscles in the back of his neck. "Because of me, she was living in sin when she died."

"We all sin, Jake, no matter how hard we try not to."

"That's just it. I wasn't trying not to."

"Was she?" she asked softly.

He had never considered it in that light. "No. She was very independent and liked things the way they were."

"Did she believe in Jesus?"

"I think so. We'd talked about it a little. I guess a minister might have called her a nominal believer or a baby Christian." A lump formed in his throat. He hadn't been a baby Christian. At one time, he'd loved the Lord, been knowledgeable about the Bible and strong in his faith, doing his best to live as God taught him to.

He had failed Pam in so many ways. It was a few minutes before he could speak. "She believed in Jesus for her salvation, but she said she'd probably get to heaven by the skin of her teeth with a deathbed confession." Tears stung his eyes, but he refused to let them fall. "She didn't have time for that."

"You can't know what happened between her and God in those few minutes. Nor can we fathom the depths of His love and mercy." Sunni stepped in front of him, taking his hands in hers. "Ultimately, each of us is responsible for our own lives, our own sin and finding our own salvation. Not shooting Henderson before he shot her was a tragedy, but I think just about anybody would have hesitated given the situation."

"It still caused her death."

"No, it may have contributed to it, and that's a terrible burden to bear, but Henderson killed her. You are not responsible for how she lived or how she died, Jake. Read Hebrews, chapter four, verse sixteen. Believe God's promise and go boldly before the throne of grace and receive mercy and grace. Don't turn away from what you so desperately need."

In his heart, he knew she was right. He couldn't continue the way he had, buried beneath the pain of his sorrow and guilt, hiding out at the ranch. Living in his dark, bitter world was no longer an option. Sunni's faith had illuminated that darkness, had shown him how much he had lost.

But he didn't quite know how to take those last steps. When he went before the throne of grace, it wouldn't be boldly. If he worked up the courage to crawl into God's presence, he couldn't do it in front of Sunni or anyone else. He had to do it alone.

"You've given me a lot to think about." He squeezed her hands. "I will think about it, sugar. Maybe even pray about it when I work up the courage. It's not something I can do here and now."

"I understand. You need to deal with this one to One. Don't wait too long, Jake. I hate to see you so miserable."

"And here I thought I was putting up such a good front." He gently tugged his hands free, settling one at her waist.

"You do pretty well most of the time."

He brushed his fingertips across her cheek and down her jaw. "Not until you came along. You're changing me, Sunni. Bringing back a part of me that I thought was gone forever. You've given me a glimmer of hope that somewhere, hidden beneath the rusty iron layers of the man I've become, there is still a part of the man I used to be."

She rested her hands on his shoulders. "You're a good man, Jake. You've been wonderful to me."

"I want to be like I used to be, not suspicious of everybody and their motives. Someone who looked for the good in people. The man who was gentle with kids and cats and old codgers and didn't know better than to show kindness to strangers."

"You may have become hardened and a little rusty, but that man has always been there. He's here now." She tapped his chest with her finger. "I was a stranger and you took me in. I don't think many people would have done that. Look at how you are with Drew and Cody. They adore you." She reached up and tickled his earlobe. "Of course, I don't know about the cats and old codgers because I haven't seen you with them."

"Haven't run into any lately. Reckon we'll have to try to find some and see how I do." He moved his other hand to her back and edged closer. There were so many things he wanted to say but didn't dare. He couldn't explain how he felt about her to himself. How could he possibly explain it to her?

His gaze fell on her lips. There were ways other than using words for a man to tell a woman he cherished her. And she had put her hand back on his shoulder again. She definitely wasn't telling him to keep away.

Out of the corner of his eye, he saw Licorice limping toward them. Jake dropped his hand and stepped back. "Looks like ol' dog picked up a thorn."

Sunni stepped back, looking at Licorice. "Oh, you poor baby. What happened?"

Jake jogged toward him. Licorice stopped and sat down, holding up his front paw with a whimper. Kneeling beside him, Jake examined his foot. "It's just a couple of grass burrs."

"But they hurt."

"Yes, they do." He carefully pulled the stickers from the pads on the dog's paw, checking to make sure he got everything. "There you go, buddy. Good as new."

Licorice licked his hand and lay down, panting heavily.

"He needs some water." Sunni hurried back to the ice chest. Taking out a cold bottle, she brought back it and the water dish. When Jake stood, she handed him the bottle. He twisted the cap off and poured the water into the bowl. She set it down right in front of the dog. Licorice drank greedily, downing practically all of it in a couple of minutes.

"It's getting hotter. Maybe we should head back home, see the rest of the ranch another day." She patted Licorice on the head. "That black fur soaks up the sun, doesn't it, baby dog?"

Jake wished she'd talk to him in that sweet, crooning voice. "When you went to get the water, he told me that he was ready for another piece of Aunt Lynda's pie."

"He didn't have a piece of pie. Only a couple of bites."

"Well, there you go. No wonder he's complaining. Poor dog was deprived of sustenance."

Laughing, Sunni waited as Jake picked up the water dish and retrieved the cooler. "So, tell me, cowboy, why is it that every time Licorice says he's hungry, you're the one who winds up with food?"

"Somebody has to provide the nibbles."

CHAPTER NINE

That night, long after Sunni and Lynda were asleep and Licorice snored softly on his doggie bed in the corner, Jake lay in bed, wide-awake, staring out the window. He'd been pacing around the house earlier and still wore the navy-blue shorts and gray T-shirt that he had changed into when they got back from their drive.

The stars sparkled as they did only in the vast sky of West Texas, millions of them in and around the Milky Way. They were always there, but sometimes thin clouds or even a storm blocked the view.

Like God. He was always there, steadfast in His love and faithfulness, but sometimes the clouds of sin or the storms of life obscured His presence.

Jake figured God knew him better than he knew himself — his sins, his guilt and shame, his grief. He had quietly gone through the long list, laying them one by one on the altar before the Lord. Tears rolling down his cheeks, he slid off the bed onto his knees and leaned forward, resting his forearms on the floor and his face on his arms. Broken in spirit and contrite of heart, he whispered, "Merciful God, please forgive me. Take me back. Make me whole."

Licorice stirred and walked over to him. Lying down, the dog nudged his arm with his nose, showing his concern.

"It's okay, boy. I'm just talkin' to God. I don't suppose you've ever heard me do that." His leg began to ache, and he gave up physically kneeling before the Lord. As he leaned back against the side of the bed, stretching his leg out in front of him, he trusted God to understand that his heart and soul were still bowed before Him.

Licorice laid his head on his lap, and Jake absently smoothed his hand along the dog's back. "Lord, thank you for washing my sins away. You know what's in my heart. You know how sorry I am for all the things I've done, and all the things I didn't do that I should have. Please guide me, Lord, help me to get it right from now on.

"Give me the faith to trust in You when I mess up or when something happens that I don't understand." He wiped the tears from his face, but new ones welled up in his eyes.

"Help me to forgive myself, especially concerning Pam's death."

He remembered something that the chaplain at the hospital had suggested a month after the shooting. Jake had chewed him out, saying things that he was ashamed of. Now, he realized the man had been right. "Help me to forgive Pam for yelling at Henderson, for drawing his fire." He took a deep breath. "For saving me when I was the one who should have died instead of her. Help me forgive her for dying when I couldn't make amends."

There were others he needed to forgive — the people in Coyote Springs who had gossiped about him or demeaned him. A few people in Austin who had taken pleasure in his downfall. Acknowledging what he needed to do was the first step. Working it all out so the forgiveness was real in his heart and mind would take time. He hadn't expected everything to be made right in one night of prayer, but at least he wasn't fighting his battle alone anymore.

God was with him as He had always been, but now Jake had the courage and the freedom to reach out to Him. His tears had dried, the ache in his heart had lessened, and he felt God's presence and peace wrap around him. "Thank You, Lord, for Your forgiveness and mercy. Thank You, Jesus, for Your love. Guide me, especially where Sunni is concerned."

He sat there for a while, petting his dog, resting in the comfort and love of Jesus, his Savior, his Friend. He had not realized how much he had missed Him.

Yawning, he nudged Licorice. "Let's hit the hay, big guy. We've got a busy day tomorrow —" he glanced at the clock "— today."

The dog got up and sleepily headed for his bed. Halfway there, he stopped, looking at the closed door. His ears perked up, and he was instantly alert, trotting to the door.

Jake glanced at the baseball bat he kept beside the bed. Lic hadn't growled, so he didn't think there was any danger. He left the bat where it was and followed the dog to the door, easing it open.

Lic ran the short distance down the hall to Sunni's room, pushing against the door with his nose, but it didn't budge. Jake was right behind him. He could hear Sunni's moans and whimpers through the closed door. Another nightmare. Jake opened the door, grabbing Licorice by the collar when the dog started to charge into the room. "Wait," he whispered. "Stay right here. I'll handle it."

With a little grumble, the dog sat down in the hallway, watching Sunni intently.

Barefoot, Jake walked silently across the room and eased down on the edge of the bed. The night-light in the outlet beside the dresser cast a soft glow over the room. Sunni had a death grip on the top sheet. Beneath it, her legs twitched. Swinging her head side to side on the pillow and panting, she moaned again.

"Sunni, wake up. It's Jake. You're having a nightmare."

She twisted away, her muffled cries more insistent.

When she turned back toward him, he touched her shoulder. "Come on, Sunni, wake up."

Gasping, her eyes flew open and she bolted upright, pummeling him with her fists.

"Sunni, wake up!" He grabbed her wrists, dodging when she jerked one free and swung her hand at him. He caught it and pulled her against his chest, then wrapped his arms around her back, holding her tightly against him. She tried to pull free, and he spoke softly, almost directly into her ear. "Sunni, it's Jake. Wake up, sweetheart. You're safe. Nobody's going to hurt you."

She struggled for a few seconds, then her

body went limp. She leaned her forehead on his shoulder, breathing hard and fast.

Jake loosened his hold, allowing her to unclench her fists and spread her fingers against his chest. He slowly moved his hand up and down her back, trying to soothe her. "Bad one, huh?"

She nodded, her hair brushing the side of his face, tangling in the stubble of his beard. "Couldn't get away from them. Couldn't stop running." Taking a deep breath, she pulled her hands from between them and slid them around his back. Turning her head, she rested the side of her face on his shoulder. "Dodging bullets."

Jake frowned and tightened his arms minutely. "Different dream?"

"Partly like the old one but mostly different. This time it started with me in the city on the sidewalk, holding the hurt man. He'd been shot. I figured that out a couple of dreams ago."

He wondered why she hadn't told him about it. "Do you know who it is?"

A deep breath shuddered through her. "This time it was you."

"Because of what I told you yesterday. Sunni, I'm sorry. I shouldn't have gone into such detail."

"I don't think it would have mattered. Just

the thought of you being hurt so bad breaks my heart. Then I was running through the pasture, but this time, instead of animals chasing me, it was two men. And they were shooting at me."

He drew back so he could look at her face. "Men from the city? Did they shoot the man on the sidewalk?" Was this a memory twisted into her nightmare?

"I don't know." She shrugged. "But they weren't wearing cowboy boots. Tennis shoes, jeans and big, loose T-shirts with pictures of cars on the front."

He relaxed a little. "Like the guys in that movie we watched for about half an hour last night? Before they robbed the convenience store and got away on their skateboards?"

"I'm not sure they were the same, but very similar. That's probably where they came from. The guys in the movie were shooting at people, too." She gave him a halfhearted, wobbly smile. "It must be hard to fire a gun from a skateboard."

"You can fire a gun from almost anywhere. Hitting what you want to is another story." Using both hands, he brushed her hair back from her face. "Are you okay now?"

"Yes. I may not go back to sleep for a while, but I'm not shaking anymore."

"Heavenly Father, be with Sunni the rest of tonight. Help her to relax and go back to sleep. Keep away the nightmares and give her Your peace. In Jesus' name, amen."

She looked up at him in wonder. "You just prayed."

"Felt good, too. I don't think it bounced off the ceiling, either, because I've been talking to God for the last couple of hours. Dug up the communication line and got most of the kinks out."

She hugged him. "I'm so glad."

"Me, too." He glanced toward the doorway. Licorice had finally given up and lain down. His head rested on his paws, but he watched them. "Come here, Lic. See for yourself that she's all right."

Licorice walked over to Sunni and sat, nudging her hand when she reached down to pet him. He ignored Jake.

"He heard you, led me to you."

"You're such a good boy." She scratched him beneath the collar.

Jake thought he heard his dog purr. "Come on, Lic. Let's get to bed." When he stood, the dog did, too. "You don't have to go with us today, Sunni. If you want to keep sleeping, go right ahead."

"And miss seeing a couple of real cowboys

in action? No way. Don't you dare let me oversleep."

"Yes, ma'am. See you at five or there-abouts." He could function on four-and-a-half hours' sleep. He'd done it plenty of times in the past.

"I'll stagger out. Just make sure the coffee's ready." She stuffed a pillow behind her and pulled the sheet a little higher.

He wondered if she'd had a sudden twinge of modesty. There was no need. Between her purple print pajamas and the dim light, he hadn't seen anything he shouldn't have.

"Coffeepot is all ready to turn on." He edged toward the door.

"Do you have a camera?"

"Yes, a great 35mm that I used when I was with the Rangers." He waited for the pain that usually hit him at the mention — or thought — of the job he had once loved. It came, but it was more of a low-key ache rather than a violent jab. God was working already. *Thank You, Lord.*

"I'd like to take some pictures of you herding the cattle. Mementos to treasure when I leave."

His heart skipped a beat. "You thinkin' of vacating the premises anytime soon?"

"No." Her soft laughter sounded hollow in the near-darkness. "I'd be terrified to go anywhere else. How could I? I don't have a job or any money. I may not know who I am, but I am aware that it takes money to buy food and put a roof over a person's head. Unless that person keeps sponging off others."

"You don't eat much." He tried to make his voice light and teasing. "And the roof would be here whether you were or not."

"But I need to contribute, earn my way. I don't want to be a freeloader."

He went back to the bed and sat down again, clasping her hand. This was becoming a habit. A dangerous one. "Sunni, you aren't a freeloader. You've been healing from an ordeal that could have killed you."

"I'm not recovering anymore. I'm fine. Well, except for all the personal blank space in my brain, but that shouldn't affect my ability to work."

"We'll think on it. See if we can come up with something for you to do. I understand your need to keep busy and to be able to provide for yourself." He wished he could tell her that she didn't have to worry, that he'd take care of her forever. *Where did that come from?*

He released her hand and stood again, hoping he made it back to his room this time. "I've got to get some sleep or I'm liable to fall off my horse about midmorning."

"Thank you, Jake." She leaned over and looked past him. "You, too, Licorice, wherever you are."

"He's gone on to bed."

"Smart dog."

Jake chuckled. "Sometimes I think he's smarter than all of us clumped together."

Carrying a travel mug with her second cup of coffee, Sunni walked over to the corral fence to watch Jake saddle Caz in the dawning light. His pickup sat nearby with a two-horse trailer attached. Licorice lay beside it. He stretched, raised his head and plopped it back down with a yawn.

Jake's camera hung from a strap around her neck. Another strap, attached to a bag holding film and various accessories, was hooked over her shoulder. The camera wasn't the most expensive she'd seen in ads on television or the Internet, but it was nice, with lots of bells and whistles, including separate zoom and wide-angle lenses.

When he had shown her how to use it after breakfast, it quickly became obvious that she was very familiar with cameras. It only took her a few minutes to grasp things that he said took him a week to understand.

Having the camera comforted her in an odd being-with-an-old-friend sort of way. Perhaps Jake and the sheriff were right when they speculated that she had stopped along the highway to take some pictures before she became lost.

Jake lifted the saddle onto the horse's back, talking quietly, telling Caz about what they would be doing that day. He hadn't noticed Sunni's presence, and she didn't mind a bit. She wasn't finished staring at him.

Oh, he looks fine this morning. Dusty, sweat-stained, wide-brimmed straw hat turned up high on each side. Long-sleeved lightweight denim Western shirt. Jeans tucked into his boots, the opposite of how he usually wore them. Spurs fastened around his boots, jingling softly when he moved. Heavy leather chaps fastened around his waist and covering his legs. The epitome of a working West Texas cowboy.

As quietly as possible, she set the cup on top of a corral post and slipped the bag strap off her shoulder, setting it on the ground. Bending her knees slightly put her at the right height to peer between the boards on the fence. The first rays of morning sunshine were behind them, with Caz blocking the sun, silhouetting Jake and his horse in a diffused golden backlight.

Raising the camera, she adjusted the lens, glad she'd had the foresight to attach the zoom before she left the house. One more tiny twist brought man and animal into focus and centered in the middle of the picture. *Click.* Caz twitched his ears, but Jake didn't seem to notice. He'd quit talking and was humming an old hymn.

Smiling, Sunni tiptoed over a couple of steps. *Click.* Jake shifted from humming to singing quietly in a beautiful baritone. Any church choir would nab him in a second. Did Kincaid Community have a choir? She should ask. She'd discovered on Sunday that her singing voice wasn't too bad. Not as good as Jake's, but maybe a church that small would welcome a willing choir participant who simply could carry a tune.

The sunlight glinted through Caz's mane, turning it to golden fire. Sunni zoomed in on the horse's neck and head, shifted slightly for a better angle and captured the shot. Lowering the camera, she contemplated what had just happened. It would be a fantastic photograph. She'd recognized the potential shot and reacted immediately, operating the camera without conscious thought.

A shiver swept over her. Would an amateur

photographer respond that quickly, acting instinctively? She didn't think so.

Moving back a few steps along the fence, Sunni stayed in the shadow as the full sunlight hit Jake and his horse. She focused the camera on Jake as he tightened the cinch. She took that picture and one more when he straightened. Then she zoomed in on his face and called softly, "Hey, handsome."

He looked toward her with a smile so tender, so welcoming, that her breath caught in her throat. Her mind and body went on photographer autopilot. *Click.* Good thing, too. If she'd had to consciously think about pressing that button — an impossibility when he looked at her that way — she wouldn't have gotten a picture to treasure forever.

"Mornin', sunshine." Leading Caz, he walked toward her, spurs jingling musically. "Tryin' to break my camera?"

"By taking your picture?" When he nodded, Sunni laughed. "I think I'll do a cowboy calendar featuring Jake Trayner. Sell it on the Internet and get rich in no time."

"More likely, you'd have a thousand calendars and no takers." Jake grinned and opened the corral gate. "I suppose folks could tack 'em to a tree and use them for shooting practice. My nose would make a good bull's-eye."

"You have a nice nose." And gorgeous eyes. A strong jaw. Firm chin. And a perfect mouth. Longing, both physical and emotional, swept through her.

"Sugar, you got lousy timing."

Startled, she looked up, reading what she'd been thinking in his eyes. "I do?"

"Unless you don't mind an audience."

A small cloud of dust on the road drew her attention. The pickup pulling a horse trailer slowed and turned into the driveway leading past the house to the corrals. "Oh. Right. Lousy timing." She stepped back and watched Caleb and his family drive up. "That's a big trailer."

"They're bringing three horses." Jake led Caz though the open gate. "Caleb and I decided last night that the boys could help us."

"Aren't they a little young for work?"

"Not on a ranch. I started helping my dad when I was about Cody's age. Moving the cattle today should be fairly simple. It's good experience for them. Besides, anytime those two get to ride horses, they think it's fun, not work."

"How about the big boys? Do you and Caleb think it's fun?"

"Of course." Jake grinned and waved at his neighbors. "Work, too, but enjoyable." He rubbed Caz's neck. "Especially when you have a good horse. If you decide you want to give riding a try, let me know."

He'd made the offer before, but Sunni couldn't seem to work up the courage to do it. "I don't know why the thought of being up there by myself scares me silly."

"Could be related to your fall in some way. There's no need to push it."

Caleb climbed out of his truck. "You ready to load up?" At Jake's nod, he walked to the back of Jake's trailer and lowered the tailgate, forming a ramp.

Sunni grabbed the camera bag and her coffee, following Jake and Caz.

Jake led the horse up the ramp into the trailer. Caleb dropped a bar behind Caz so he couldn't back out. Jake tied the reins to a hook and exited through a side door. Caleb lifted the tailgate and closed it securely. They had obviously done this many times before.

As Caleb walked back to his pickup, Jake opened the passenger door on his truck for Sunni, smiling mischievously. "Need a boost?"

"I can make it if you hold my coffee cup."

He leaned closer and murmured into her

ear, "I'd rather hold you."

Sunni blinked and looked up at him as he straightened. His eyes twinkled, but they were a darker blue than normal. She turned toward him, holding out the mug. "You might as well take the coffee and dump it out 'cause now I'm wide-awake."

He chuckled and took the cup from her hand, setting it on the edge of the truck bed. "Just think how charged up you'd be if I lifted you up to the seat and gave you a good-morning kiss."

She didn't dare think about it, so she laughed. "No doubt Megan would love it." *And so would I.* "Focus on the job at hand, cowboy."

"I am, which right now is flirting with you." He gave her that lazy grin, the one that turned her knees to jelly but somehow made everything seem all right anyway.

"Well, I have to admit, you have that task down perfectly."

His whole face lit up. "Not just good but perfect?"

"Oh, great. Now you're going to have to buy a bigger hat."

"Justified expense."

Caleb leaned out the truck window with a grin. "Quit wastin' daylight, Trayner." He started the engine.

"Tell that sister of yours to teach you some manners."

Before Sunni had a chance to turn around toward the truck, Jake gripped her waist and lifted her up on the seat. She held her breath, half hoping he'd kiss her, half hoping he wouldn't. Not in front of the others.

He didn't.

She didn't know whether to be disappointed or relieved.

CHAPTER TEN

The road made a big circle, leading them back past the house. Caleb pulled in behind them. They went in the general direction of the old house where Jake's grandparents had lived but turned south before they reached it. After about five minutes, Sunni's racing pulse and the tension hovering between them eased.

"I think I got some good pictures of you and Caz this morning."

Jake glanced at her, slowing as a roadrunner raced down the dirt road ahead of them. "You'd taken some before I saw you?"

She nodded. "Several. By the way, you have a great voice. I can't wait to hear you singing in church."

His expression softened. "This morning was the first time I've felt like singing in over two years. A little gift from God, I think."

"He put a song in your heart."

"That's right, one of thanksgiving." A trace of huskiness edged his voice. "I can't tell you how good it felt."

"You don't have to. I could hear it and see it in your face."

"So tell me about the pictures." He turned down another road. Grass and weeds were about a foot high in the space between the tire tracks.

Sunni briefly described the shots, not wanting to brag on them too much until she saw the actual prints in case they weren't as great as she thought they would be. Maybe she was too impressed with herself. Perhaps anybody who had dabbled with photography, taking lots of family or vacation photos, could have done as well. When they were developed, she'd probably discover that she had cut off the top of Jake's head like the guy did in the TV commercial.

"It will be fun to see them. Feel free to take as many today as you want. There are three more rolls of film in the bag. I had planned to use them on my next Ranger assignment, checking out an oddball cult commune that we suspected was a front for a drug-smuggling operation."

"Do you miss being with the Rangers?"

"Sometimes. But I'll never try to go back.

I doubt they'd let me for one thing. To be honest, I don't have the confidence that I used to have. I'd always worry about doing something wrong and my partner getting hurt. Or I'd get hurt. I'd just as soon not put myself in that situation again. Maybe that's cowardly, but that's the way it is, so I have to accept it."

"I don't think it's cowardly. You served in law enforcement for a long time. I don't think it has to be a lifelong commitment. Now it's time for something else."

"I'm glad you feel that way. I enjoy ranching and living out here. There isn't the security of a regular paycheck, but my books are in the black." He smiled ruefully. "This year at least. I'll never be rich, but I'm happy." He glanced at her and added softly, "Especially now."

Now. Because he'd restored his relationship with God. That was a certainty. Because she was with him? She hoped, perhaps foolishly, that she contributed to his happiness. *Lord, no matter what happens, whether or not I regain my memory, please don't let me hurt him.*

Jake stopped the pickup in front of a gate made of barbed wire, like the fence. When he got out to open it, Sunni watched the procedure with interest. A loop of wire attached to the fence post went over the top of the gate post. Another circled the bottom. He pushed the gate post toward the fence until he could slip the wire loop off over the top. Then he picked up the gate post, lifting the bottom free of the second loop and dragged the gate over to the side. The gate had been pulled taut to begin with, and though Jake made it look easy, she suspected it would have been a challenge if she tried it.

The land was gently rolling and open, with fewer mesquites than she had seen on other parts of the ranch. About ten cows plus their calves grazed in the area visible from the truck. At the sound of the vehicles and trailers, several of them lifted their heads, watching the intruders suspiciously.

He climbed back inside the truck, drove into the pasture and parked, leaving room for Caleb to pull his rig in beside him. "We'll unload the horses here. We'll move the cattle east, to the other side of the pasture, and open the gate. Let them stroll on through to their next buffet. You and Megan follow along in my truck so you can watch and pick up the boys and their horses if they get tired."

"Is Megan driving?"

He shifted to Park and turned off the

engine. "I'll leave that up to you ladies to decide. I figured you'd want her to drive so you could take pictures."

Sunni chuckled as they got out of the pickup. "Well, that's one reason. I don't think I want to attempt to drive this monster truck of yours for the first time pulling a trailer."

"Hey, it's not a monster truck." He let Licorice out and met her at the back of the trailer. "The wheels aren't taller than you are."

"True. But I'd better take a test drive when you're along in case I run into a tree or something." She scanned the pasture. "Though I could probably just mow most of them down and not worry about it."

Laughing, he walked back to close the gate. "You know, I hadn't thought about that. Maybe that's the way to get rid of these mesquites."

Cody and Drew scrambled from their pickup, running over to greet Sunni. They were carbon copies of Jake and Caleb — boots, jeans, leather belts, Western shirts, chaps and straw hats. Only their outfits still had a fairly new look where the men's were well worn and well used.

"Did Uncle Jake tell you Drew and me are gonna get to help?" asked Cody with an excited grin.

"He did." She hugged him to her side. The sweetness of the little boy wrapped around her heart. Sunni wasn't surprised by the longing she felt. She'd experienced it every time she'd been around Cody and Drew. Once again, she wondered if she had a precious child somewhere, waiting for her to come home.

If not, would she someday have a little cowboy of her own? She looked up to find Jake watching her and Cody, his expression mirroring the emotions she felt. *Lord, am I wanting what I can't have?*

Heart racing, she tore her gaze away from his, focusing on Cody. "I bet you'll be a big help to them, too. Do you have your very own horse?"

"Uh-huh. Gypsy. She's as sweet and easygoing a horse as you'll ever meet. She's the gray one that Uncle Caleb is unloading."

Sunni wondered which grown-up had made that proclamation. "She's pretty. Drew, what's your horse's name?" She watched as Megan took Gypsy's reins from Caleb and led her around to the side of the trailer.

"Willow. She's a bay. She's pretty easygoing, too. That's her backing out of the trailer now. I'd better go help." Drew walked over to his uncle, taking the reins and leading her out of the way.

The last horse out of Caleb's trailer was a big palomino. Out of the corner of her eye, Sunni saw that Jake had Caz out of his trailer.

"That's Uncle Caleb's horse, Prince."

"He's beautiful, too. Kinda big though."

"Yeah, he's a little bigger 'cause Uncle Caleb's a little bigger than us."

"That makes sense." She supposed. To her, Gypsy and Willow looked much too large for such little boys.

"I gotta go." Cody started toward his horse, then stopped and looked back at Sunni. "You're gonna watch us, aren't you?"

"Yes, sir. I'll even try to get some pictures of you at work."

"Cool!" When he turned, Sunni expected him to go racing over to his mom and Gypsy, but he walked carefully up to the horse, talking to the mare as Megan handed him the reins.

Jake led Caz over to where Sunni stood. "Caz wants to keep you company while I help the kids mount."

"He does, does he?" Sunni rubbed the horse's neck. She wasn't afraid of him as long as her feet were firmly planted on the ground. She took the reins from Jake, murmuring sweet nothings to the horse.

Standing on the other side of Caz, Jake watched her with a bemused expression, then shook his head. "How do you do that?"

"What?"

"Make me jealous of a horse."

"Somehow calling you a pretty boy doesn't quite cut it."

Jake grinned and swatted at a fly that buzzed his ear. "Guess not."

"Gorgeous hunk is more appropriate."

His grin turned smug. "Yeah?"

"Yeah." She glanced behind him. Caleb was lifting Drew into the saddle. "If you're going to help the kids, you'd better get a move on, darlin'." She hadn't purposely spoken with a little Texas twang, but it came out anyway.

Jake's eyes locked with hers, and he trailed his fingertip along her cheek. "Yes, ma'am."

He turned and walked over to Cody. Sunni picked up the camera, then promptly released it, letting it hang by the strap. Her hands were shaking so much that if she took a picture right then, everybody would think they'd had an earthquake.

Jake got Cody settled on Gypsy, talked to Megan and Caleb for a few minutes, then came back for Caz. Pulling on his gloves, he took the reins in one hand. "Time to get to work. I'll see you when we take a break to eat. Have fun."

"You, too."

"Chasin' cows on a horse is always fun." He paused for a second, searching her eyes, then mumbled, "Aw, why not."

Curling his hand around the back of her neck, he leaned down and gave her a quick, firm kiss.

And sent her senses reeling.

He released her and held her gaze for moment. Then he guided Caz back a few steps and mounted.

She stared at him as he rode over to join the others. The boys snickered. Caleb lifted his eyebrows in amusement, and Megan grinned.

Sunni didn't care. The man had taken her breath away, and it had little to do with being caught by surprise. That kiss and the promise she'd seen in his eyes left her dazed. Passion. Tenderness. Love? Did she only see what she wanted to? The reflection of her own heart?

"Wait a minute," called Megan. "Let me take a picture of y'all before you get all dirty."

Sunni blinked, noting that the guys had lined up, Jake and Caleb on the outside with the boys in the middle. Pulling off the lens cap and stuffing it in her pocket, she moved closer to Megan, framing all four horses and riders in the picture.

"Y'all say cheese."

"Cheese!" The boys yelled it out and grinned. The men just smiled. It was a good one. She quickly adjusted the lens, zooming in on the boys, taking their picture as they teased each other about their cheesy smiles. Another tweak of the lens for one of Caleb as he turned his horse away. Then Jake . . . who watched her thoughtfully. She snapped the picture anyway, then lowered the camera, feeling a little self-conscious.

"Wow." Megan stared at her, her eyes wide.

"What did I do?" Frowning, Sunni's gaze shifted between Megan and Jake as he walked the horse toward her.

"You just took a gazillion pictures," said Megan.

Sunni laughed and replaced the lens cap. "It was only four."

The saddle leather creaked as Jake leaned forward and rested his hands on the saddle horn. "Different subjects, different focal lengths, rapid shots. You work like a professional, Sunni."

"Really?" Excitement spiraled through

her. "I think I got some good ones this morning, but I figured maybe I've just taken a lot of vacation photos or something. This camera is so easy to use, it seems like anybody could just snap away and get great pictures."

"Believe me, they can't. I used that camera for a year, and though I became proficient with it, I was never able to operate it the way you just did. I suppose confirmation will be how the pictures turn out."

"Do they have a one-hour photo in Coyote Springs?"

"Waylon Cummings does film processing. I expect he'd do it fast for us. He also does digital scanning and printing. He has an Internet site. People send him photos from all across the country for special printing. He also sometimes fills in as photographer for the newspaper and does wedding photos." Jake looked over his shoulder. Caleb and the boys were already rounding up some cows. "I'd better go to work before Caleb gets on my case again.

"Ladies." He gave them a brief nod, touching the front brim of his hat with his fingertips and thumb just like the handsome hero in the Western they'd watched several nights earlier.

Sunni sighed as he turned Caz and trotted away. "I think I may swoon."

Megan giggled. "He wasn't hamming it up. Cowboys really do that. I see it all the time in Coyote Springs when I walk down the street."

"But do they do the same to the little old ladies?"

"Some do." Megan grinned as they started toward the pickup. "But some don't. When they stop, I'll know I'm getting old."

Megan had no problem handling Jake's truck. They drove through the pasture behind the cowboys for a while, then eased on ahead so they could stop and watch the action. "Let's get in the back, so we have a better view all the way around." She parked in the slight shade of a mesquite, and they climbed up in the pickup bed, sitting on the side for a few minutes.

Sunni spotted Jake coming out of some brush, herding a cow and calf. "Is it okay if I stand?"

"Should be all right if you don't make any sudden movements."

She slowly stood, leaning against the cab and took their picture. A few minutes later, the cow took off at a run and tried to go back into the brush, but Jake and Caz raced alongside and cut her off. Sunni snapped half-a-dozen shots, being careful not to do anything that might spook the cow or the horse.

Then the boys came into view, herding about fifteen cows and their calves in a tight group at a slow but steady pace. If an animal tried to break away, one of the boys quickly got her back in place.

Sunni watched them for a few minutes. "They're amazing."

"Aren't they? I'm thrilled that they've taken to ranching so quickly and so well. Of course, they may change their minds when they get older, but I hope not. Caleb would love for them to follow in his footsteps and actually run things."

Sunni took several pictures. "What if they want to do something else? Be a lawyer or a doctor or a Wall Street stockbroker?"

"I'll do everything I can to help them follow their dreams. Caleb, too. Although we might try to talk them out of moving clear to New York.

"Grandpa left the ranch to Caleb. Dad is a high-powered businessman in Dallas. Grandpa knew that if Dad inherited it, he'd sell it. My ex-husband cleaned out our bank accounts and mortgaged the house to the hilt, then left me for his old high school sweetheart when I was pregnant with Cody. Caleb offered to let us live here, and we've been here ever since. He made me a partner in the ranch a couple of years ago. Things will be different if he gets married and has a family of his own. There will be more issues to sort out then."

The day went well, with the cattle cooperating for the most part. Though the boys were worn-out by the time the last cow and calf were ushered into the new pasture, their pride and sense of accomplishment beamed on their faces. Sunni doubted that Cody and Drew would ever seek life in the big city. They loved ranch life and West Texas too much to leave.

As did she. Her focus drifted to Jake as he helped Cody unsaddle Gypsy. Her heart whispered that it wasn't just the ranch and land that she loved. It was the man. She didn't know how she could have fallen in love in two weeks. Since they were together most of the time, perhaps that was the rough equivalent of a month or two of normal dating.

Please, God, don't make me have to choose between him and someone else.

After a delicious supper cooked by Sunni, Jake helped with the cleanup, then sprawled in his brown leather recliner. Lynda sat in the rocker with her feet on the hassock, studying the main local competition to her store — the new fall JC Penney catalog. Sunni was curled up on the couch thumbing through a new women's magazine that Lynda had brought home for her.

A month earlier, before his aunt moved in, he and Licorice would have been by themselves, both snoring after sharing a frozen dinner. One definite advantage to having women around, at least the two currently bunking at his place, was that the meals had greatly improved. When they both went back to their normal lives — a thought that threatened to ruin his evening, especially relating to Sunni — he'd have to do a better job of cooking for himself than he had in the past.

"Did you find the recipe for that peach-chicken stuff in one of my cookbooks?"

Lynda snorted. "What cookbooks?"

Jake rolled his eyes. "Okay, one of my mom's cookbooks."

Sunni chuckled at them and laid the magazine down on her lap. "No. Actually, I haven't seen any cookbooks around here."

"They're on a shelf in the hall closet. I never use them and didn't like them cluttering up the counter." That was only partially the truth. He hadn't been able to bear looking at them after his mom died. She had loved cooking and regularly won blue ribbons at the county fair for her creations.

"Do you mind if I dig them out?"

Sunni's question caught him by surprise, but not as much as his reaction to it. As long as she was the one using them, the thought of seeing them again didn't bother him. His throat tightened, and he cleared it, noting Lynda's swift and knowing glance. "No, I don't mind. I think my mom would be pleased if someone put them to good use."

"Thanks. I got the chicken recipe off the Internet. It's so easy even you could do it."

"You think?" He smiled, enjoying her teasing.

"Yep. Put some chicken in pan, sprinkle with salt and pepper. Add a little lemon juice to the peach juice, pour it over the chicken and bake for about half an hour. Add the peaches and bake about fifteen minutes longer."

"That's it?" When she nodded, he asked, "Did you print it out?"

"Yes. I stuck it in the pantry next to the flour canister, along with several others I want to try."

"Go for it. I'll gladly be your guinea pig."

When the phone rang, he picked up the cordless lying on the table by his chair and answered it. "Evenin', Toby." Jake winked at his aunt as she plunked the catalog on the floor. "Any new leads?"

"Not a thing," said Toby. "There was another pickup stolen from the side of the highway about fifteen miles out of Robert Lee, but they got away clean. I don't understand it. They just seem to vanish into thin air."

"Probably stripped out for parts by now."

"This one was brand-new. The guy drove it off the lot last week. My gut tells me that if we ever catch these guys, we might find out something about Sunni. How's she doin'?"

"Fine." Jake's gaze lingered on her face. She lifted one nicely arched brow and mouthed, *Anything?* He shook his head. Sighing, she picked up the magazine again. "Caleb and the boys and I showed her how to move cattle today. I think she had fun taking pictures." She glanced up, smiled and nodded. "She seems to have a knack for it."

"Maybe I'll hire her to take mug shots of the prisoners when we book 'em for jail."

Jake laughed and lowered the footrest on the recliner. "You'd better pay her by the hour. If you hire it out as piecework, she wouldn't make enough to cover the gas to get to town."

"Don't knock our peaceful county, son. Is Lynda there?"

"I'm handing her the phone right now." Jake stood, holding the phone out to his aunt, grinning when she all but jerked it out of his hand.

He turned to Sunni. "I'm going to take some carrots down to the horses. Want to go?"

"Sure." She slid her feet into her sandals and stood, following him into the kitchen.

He noticed that Lynda had started to get up, but when she saw they were leaving, she settled back into her chair. Jake took a handful of carrots from the bag in the refrigerator and put the rest away. Before they started out the back door, he peeked around the corner at his aunt. She was resting her head against the back of the rocker, wearing a dreamy smile.

"I suppose we shouldn't hurry back." He opened the door leading to the screen porch, waiting for Sunni to go ahead of him.

"Fine with me. It's a lovely evening."

Jake waited for Licorice to go out with them, then closed the door quietly. They crossed the porch and stepped outside. Carrying the carrots in one hand, he reached for Sunni's hand with the other, his heart warming as she curled her fingers around his.

"Did you get a chance to talk to Lynda about working at the store?"

"Yes. She wants me to start next Monday. She said they could use me two days a week. I think I'll enjoy it, but I feel guilty about them paying me. After all you both have done for me, I should work for free."

"Then you wouldn't earn any money, and you'd still feel as if you didn't have an option to staying here. Besides, Lynda doesn't operate that way. If she pays someone to work and they don't do a good job, she can fire them and that's the end of it. They go look for other employment because they need the money. But if they volunteer and do a lousy job, it's harder to get rid of them."

"No need for money, so no hurry to look for something else."

"Right. She tried it once, and the woman made one mistake after another. But she insisted on staying, saying that she could learn. And she did try, but it was hopeless. Finally, she boxed up a whole shipment of new clothes and took them to the local mission instead of the clearance items she was supposed to give away. Lynda had to insist that she not come back and help anymore. They couldn't afford it."

"Yikes. I hope I don't do something like that."

"You won't. You have too much common sense."

"Which seems odd when you think about it. You'd think my memories, the things I've been taught or learned in life would make me that way."

"Maybe all that runs on another wavelength. Kind of under the conscious personal memory radar so to speak, tying in with the knowledge and skills memory."

"I think I'll ask Dr. Smith about that the next time we talk."

When they reached the corral, Caz and Prancer were waiting for them by the fence.

"Y'all thought we'd never get here, didn't you?" Jake gave half the carrots to Sunni, then held one through the fence to Caz. She did the same for Prancer. Prancer snorted at Jake, then took the carrot. "Now, girl, you know I had to give Caz his turn to work today. Next time, you'll get to go." He handed another carrot to Caz, while Sunni waited for Prancer to finish her first one. "You'll note, being a lady, she's a more delicate eater."

"He does gobble them down."

Delicate eater or not, it didn't take the horses long to polish off the carrots. Sunni looked up at Jake. "Now what? Do they need some oats or something?"

"They already ate. That was just a treat." He draped his arm across her shoulders. "Let's take a little walk. The bench in the fruit orchard is a great place to watch the sunset."

She put her arm around his waist, and they strolled the thirty yards to the orchard, chatting about their plans for the next day. When they sat down on the bench, Sunni took a deep breath. "Those peaches smell heavenly. Are they ripe?"

"Not quite. I'm guessing another week. The plums are ripe." He turned and looked at a tree nearby, loaded with dark purple plums. "Some have already fallen on the ground. If we get a chance tomorrow, we should come pick them."

"Should I go back to the house and get a bucket or something so we can do it now?"

"No. We'd run out of sunlight." He pointed to the pink and lavender streaking across the western sky, highlighting a few puffy clouds on the horizon. "And miss the show." He put his arm around her, tucking her close up against him. "My daddy used to say that God made sunsets so we would stop, rest a spell, and contemplate all the good things the Lord has given us, starting with the beautiful painting in the sky."

"I wish I could have met your parents."

"I wish you could have, too. I think you'd have liked them. They would have adored you."

"How can you know that?" She rested her head on his arm and looked up at him.

"Because we saw things much the same way." He turned toward her, tracing his fingertips along her cheek and down the side of her neck. "And I'm crazy about you." In love with her was more the truth, but she'd probably think he was crazy — in the insane sense of the word — if he told her. Was there really such a thing as love at first sight? He was beginning to think so.

She searched his eyes, looking into his heart and soul. "You don't know me. I don't know me. What if I'm an ax murderer or something?"

He skimmed his thumb lightly across her lips, hiding a pleased smile when she shivered. "You couldn't be. Even without your memory, if you were an evil person, it would show. And I do know you. You're the woman who brought light and happiness to my dark, lonely heart. You're the woman who made me want to live life instead of just make it through one more day. You made me care again, Sunni. No matter what happens, no matter where we end up, I'll always be grateful for that and thankful to know you."

"Then it's all been worth it. I'm crazy about you, too. I care so much for you, so much more than is wise."

Would she welcome another kiss? Probably . . . at the moment. But then she'd think about the guy she remembered from the softball game, and she'd worry about possibly betraying a sacred vow. As would he. He'd thought about it off and on all day, wondering if he'd been way out of line earlier.

Jake shifted again, leaning back against the bench but keeping his arm around her shoulders. He couldn't bring himself to completely move away from her. Besides, she still needed a place to rest her head.

"It's hard to be wise." His voice sounded husky.

"Impossible on our own," she said quietly.

"Good thing the Almighty is in charge."

CHAPTER ELEVEN

Jake leaned against the truck door, resting his elbow out the open window, watching Sunni drum her fingertips against the passenger-side armrest. He'd parked in front of Cummings Graphics in the shade of a deserted building, once a nice, two-story hotel, but they were still toasty inside the pickup. Shifting his arm inside, he closed the window and started the truck.

Sunni's fingers stopped tapping. She turned to him with a scowl. "We aren't leaving."

"Just cooling off." He hit the button for the window on her side, closing it. Waylon was half an hour late, and Sunni was wound as tight as a pea vine through a picket fence. She'd been out of sorts most of the day.

"Do you think he forgot?"

"No. I expect he ran an errand and was delayed. We could go to the Dairy Queen and get something to drink."

"I'd rather stay here. I don't want to miss him." She went back to tapping and watching the street like an outlaw looking for the posse.

"Yes, ma'am." He made a mental note that Sunni did not like to be kept waiting, at least in regard to something she deemed important. Waylon had said to come back at four o'clock. Jake glanced at his watch. It was now 4:36 p.m. And Sunni was counting.

They'd dropped off three rolls of film at the shop early that morning. Waylon had shown them his top-of-the-line processor, which developed the negatives and printed the photos automatically. He could load the film, program it and walk away. Must have been a long walk.

A van turned off Second Street heading toward them. Jake nodded toward the vehicle. "That's him —" Sunni opened her door and was halfway out of the truck before he added, "Now."

He couldn't really blame her. She was waiting to discover something important about herself. Her anticipation to see her pictures from the previous day mingled with a thread of nervousness that she seldom revealed. *Please, Lord, let them be as good as she hopes. Give her this blessing.*

He rolled the windows down and turned off the ignition before climbing out to join her.

Waylon parked beside them and hurriedly got out of the van. "Sorry, folks. Had to go mediate a discussion between one of my wedding customers and her mama over her wedding photos." He unlocked the door to his building and stepped inside. Jake and Sunni followed him in, closing the door behind them. Flipping on the lights, Waylon shook his head with a snort. "Discussion, my foot. It was more like a catfight. I'm not sure whether they were really arguing or just trying to get me to give them twice as much for the money."

He turned to Sunni. "But you don't give a hoot about fussin' mamas and daughters."

Sunni managed a gracious smile, making Jake proud of her. "Well, I am anxious to see the pictures. Did you get a chance to print them?"

"Sure did. Come on back here." He led them around the counter into another room. "You're a terrific photographer."

"I am?" Sunni squeaked. She glanced at Jake and looked back to Waylon.

Jake hid a smile. He didn't think he'd ever heard that tone before.

"In a class by yourself," Waylon said

quietly. "I do fine-art print reproductions for artists and photographers from all over the country. Your work is as good as any of them and better than most." He stepped aside and motioned for them to inspect the photographs he had spread out on the worktable.

Jake scanned the pictures and let out a low whistle. He'd never seen anything like them. Action shots of him or Caleb chasing runaway cows. One of Cody spurring his horse to bring a calf back into the herd, the little boy's expression serious and determined. Even one of Licorice in midair as he jumped over a log.

Still shots, such as a perfect little baby Hereford looking straight at the camera. Another with a Longhorn mama gently nuzzling her calf. Closeups of the boys, Caleb and him right before they started the day's work.

He stared in amazement at a picture of him saddling Caz. The horse blocked the sun so they were both silhouetted against the golden rays of the sunrise. In another, focused just on Caz, the sunlight shone through Caz's mane, setting it ablaze. He hadn't known she had taken them, hadn't known she was at the corral right then.

His hand shook mildly as he picked up

the one where he first became aware of her presence at the corral. She had called to him, and his heart had rejoiced at the sound of her voice. He'd looked up, right into the camera. If she wondered about his feelings for her, she wouldn't anymore. He was a man looking at the woman he loved. Pure and simple, for all the world to see.

He laid it back on the table, tipping his head to see Sunni's reaction to her creations. She reached for the silhouette one but stopped without picking it up and drew back her trembling hand.

"I thought they'd be good," she said softly. "But I never dreamed they'd be this good." She closed her eyes, whispering, "Thank You, Jesus. Oh, thank You!"

Jake pulled her into his embrace, murmuring a heartfelt "amen" in her ear. He glanced around, noting that Waylon had slipped from the room. "You're a true artist with a camera, Sunni." He took a half step back and smoothed her hair, framing her face with both hands. "But I'm going to swipe my camera back."

"Why?" She looked so disappointed that he felt like a jerk.

"Just for a few hours. I don't have any pictures of you. They won't be as good as yours, but I've got to have some." *For when you leave me.* When she went back to the life that enabled her to capture the world as she saw it and share that unique vision with others.

"For a few hours." A teasing light glinted in her eyes. "Then I'll wrestle it back from you."

Jake chuckled and released her. "Sounds like fun. I might just take you up on that."

Waylon came back into the room carrying a box for the photos. "My niece goes to Kincaid Community Church. She sold me tickets to their barbecue a week from Saturday. They're raising funds to help the youth group go on a mission trip to Mexico."

Sunni nodded and took the box when he handed it to her. "Pastor Ron mentioned it on Sunday. People are donating things for an auction, too."

"Exactly." Waylon scanned the photos. "I'm thinking that some of these would make mighty fine items to auction off if you're so inclined. I have the best giclee printer available." He grinned at Jake. "Other guys spend their money on cows or tractors. Mine goes for the newest and greatest printing equipment. Giclee is a way of reproducing photos or paintings in a large format. It's better than lithographs, with more depth and color.

"I can do up to thirty-by-forty-inch prints, but sixteen-by-twenty inch would probably be right for the auction." He motioned toward Jake. "You have some great shots here, but you might want to include a picture or two of scenery for the auction. Get this ol' boy to show you some pretty parts of the county this week."

Excitement lit up her face. "I'd love that. It would be wonderful to contribute something, to be a part of helping the kids." A frown replaced her smile. "But I won't be able to pay you anything for about three weeks."

"I'll cover it." Jake slipped his arm around her waist. He didn't want anything to dampen her joy and enthusiasm.

"No, Jake, you've done so much already." She turned to Waylon but didn't move away from Jake. "I'm going to be working a couple of days a week at Lynda's dress shop, but I won't get paid for a while."

"Tell you what, I'll donate my costs for three prints to the cause," said Waylon. "You decide which ones you want for the auction, and I'll take it from there. But remember, we don't have a lot of time."

"That's wonderful, Waylon. Thank you."

"Gives me a way to help the other kids as well as my niece."

Sunni stepped away from Jake and started gathering up the pictures, placing them carefully in the box.

"I'm going to want some prints, too." Jake moved out of her way. "You can give me a quote on the cost once I decide which ones I want." He absently scratched a mosquito bite on the back of his forearm.

Waylon grinned, his eyes flicking between Sunni and Jake. "The hard part will be deciding."

"Ain't that the truth." He knew of probably a dozen he wanted for sure. And maybe twenty more. He didn't expect producing a fine-art print was cheap. A man could go broke having a top-notch photographer around. What was it Waylon had said? She was in a class by herself.

In plenty more ways than one.

Lynda took one look at Sunni's photos and picked up the phone. "Hi, Marcella. Are you still willing to buy out my share of the store?"

Jake met Sunni's surprised gaze and shrugged. He didn't have any idea what his aunt was up to.

"You are? Good. No, I want to think about it some more, but I'll let you know one way or the other in a few days." She listened to her friend, moving her head back and forth impatiently. "All right, hon. I'll talk to you in the morning." She hung up the phone and grinned.

"Auntie Lynda, what are you up to?" They were all in their usual places — Jake in the recliner, Sunni curled up on the couch and Lynda in the swivel rocker with her feet on the hassock. Occasionally Jake would ask if either of them wanted to sit in the recliner, the choice seat in the house as far as he was concerned, but they always declined.

"If Sunni's willing, I'm going to do something I've wanted to do for years, open an art gallery."

"Where?" Jake and Sunni asked in unison, then grinned at each other.

Lynda rolled her eyes. "In Coyote Springs, of course. In case you haven't noticed — which obviously you haven't — things are happening in town. You're excused, Sunni, because you've only been there a few times. But my nephew should get off the ranch more and take notice of the world around him."

She turned her attention to Sunni, dismissing Jake with a wave of her hand. "Four years ago, the local Chamber of Commerce came up with the idea of having the Coyote Springs Trade Days twice a year. It's basically a fair where folks come from all across West Texas and sell their crafts and artwork with a few antiques and collectibles thrown in for good measure.

"It's grown a lot the last couple of years, putting little old Coyote Springs on the map, so to speak. Not only do the people who rent booths and sell their wares profit, so do the regular merchants in Coyote Springs. A few local folks are getting brave and opening up a couple of new stores — another antiques store, and a place where people can sell their crafts year-round. The building between them is vacant, the right size for a gallery, and the rent is reasonable."

"A gallery." Sunni twisted a strand of hair around her index finger. "I'd just planned to donate some prints to the church auction."

"Which is a wonderful idea. It's for a good cause, plus it will be a great advertisement." Lynda shifted her feet from the footstool and planted them on the floor, leaning forward. "When I lived in Fort Worth, my legal secretary job paid the bills. Working in a gallery a couple of Saturdays a month saved my sanity. I know art, hon. I truly do. We had paintings and photographs, even some sculptures. A real variety. But the section that consistently sold well was Western art."

She motioned to the pictures lined up on the coffee table. Jake had been relieved to see they didn't include the one of him looking at Sunni at the corral. "Sunni, most of these are better than any photo we had in the shop. The rest are just as good. I mean it, hon. I wouldn't kid you about something that important. These will sell at the gallery and through a store Internet site. I compiled a list of customers over the years through the Fort Worth gallery. I expect I could get at least half of them to come to our grand opening."

"Surely you can't fill a whole gallery with my stuff."

Lynda laughed and leaned back in the chair, plopping her feet up on the hassock again. "No, I can't. But I know some fine West Texas artists who can use another outlet for their paintings. You'd be my only photographer, though. My prime artist."

"What about me working at the clothing store?"

"You can work in the gallery instead. I'd still pay you. And you'll get money when we sell your prints, minus the gallery commission. Don't worry about Marcella. She has two or three gals she can call to help her at the store.

"I have enough to get started and pay you a little above minimum wage even before I sell my part of the clothing store. The other artists I have in mind will leave things with us on consignment. If we want to have the store open by Trade Days, we have to start right away."

"Whew!" Sunni laughed and straightened her legs, resting her bare feet on the coffee table. "When you decide to do something, you don't wait around, do you? It sounds like a great idea, and I'd love to be a part of it. But let me think about it overnight and pray about it."

Lynda smiled and shrugged. "Guess I should do that, too. Though the good Lord knows this has been my dream for years. Things haven't been right up to now. The Bible says He gives us the desires of our hearts. I never have figured out if that means He puts the desires there in the first place or just blesses us when we come up with an idea He approves of."

"I'd like to think He does both." Sunni glanced at Jake, but unlike so many other times, he couldn't read her expression. Was she like him, wondering if God gave them the feelings they had for each other so He could bless them? Or had they come up with those on their own? If they had, would He bless their relationship anyway?

He lowered the recliner footrest. "I need to check on the horses. Want to go?" It was something he did every night, and she often went with him. He enjoyed the end of the day, but her presence made it special.

"Sure." She slipped on her shoes while he went into the kitchen for some sugar cubes.

They strolled down to the stable and gave the horses the treat.

Leaning on the fence, Sunni watched Caz and Prancer for a few minutes then glanced up at the twilight sky. "We missed the sunset."

"Can't always catch it, though I try. We could sit on the back porch for a while and watch the stars come out."

"I'd enjoy that. The second night I was lost, before I fell asleep, I lay on the ground staring up at the heavens. It comforted me to know that they were God's creation, a gift for us to enjoy, and a reminder that He was with me. I even saw a satellite go by and, a little while later, a shooting star. I told myself that others saw that same star fall, perhaps someone who wasn't all that far away. Then I didn't feel so alone."

"You were right. I saw the star but not the satellite." Jake reached through the fence and rubbed Prancer's neck. Sunni did the same to Caz.

"What were you doing awake? It must have been one or two in the morning."

"I'd had a bad dream. Came out here for a while to calm down."

She glanced at him and drew her hand back through the fence, turning toward him. "Was it about the shooting?"

"Yes." He reached over and patted Caz on the face, then turned and started back toward the house. Sunni fell in step beside him. "It's always the same, mostly the way it happened, as if my mind is on perpetual rewind and play. Except when I crawl over to Pam, she tells me I killed her and she dies. Then I wake up."

Sunni looped her arm through his. "She didn't actually say that, did she?"

"No. She couldn't speak. My guilt added that part. I've had the dream every few weeks since it happened, sometimes more. I wake up in a sweat, pulse pounding, heart aching. I'm hoping I won't have it anymore. I've begged God to take it away."

"I'll pray for that, too. Do you still believe you caused her death?"

"Yes, but not totally. I'm sharing the blame now with Henderson." And with Pam for hollering at the man. Jake didn't see any sense in bringing her into it. "I'll always have to take some of the responsibility, Sunni, because that's the way it happened. My hope now is that God can help me to forgive myself and move on. I think I'll get there, but it will take a while."

They reached the porch and went inside the screened area, safe from the bugs but open to the evening breeze. Sunni sat in one of the cushioned lawn chairs. He pulled another chair closer to her and plopped down with a contented sigh. "What do you think about Lynda's gallery idea?"

"I'm excited about it. But what happens when my memory comes back? I may already have a job somewhere."

Somewhere that might be a thousand miles away, complete with a house, a husband, two kids and a dog. Considering how much she loved animals, he probably should throw in a cat and a goldfish. Jake didn't say it, but he figured she was thinking along the same lines. "Lynda will find someone to help her run it, but she'd want you to supply her with pictures for the next thirty years."

"If I keep having as much fun as I did yesterday, then I'd do it. But she wants Western photos. What if I live in New York City?"

"You could always put a great big cowboy hat on the Statue of Liberty."

"You aren't being much help here." But she smiled. "Maybe I could persuade the Stetson company to do it as a promotional gimmick."

"There you go. Already thinking like an entrepreneur. You and Lynda will make a perfect team."

"I don't want to let her down."

"Worrying about those kinds of what-ifs will only keep you from what could be. If this is something you want to do, and God gives you peace about it, go for it. The plan can always be adjusted if necessary."

"It would be a challenge, a chance to see if I have any business skills to go along with takin' purty pictures." She waggled her eyebrows, making him laugh. "I think I would enjoy it much more than working in the clothing store. I was a little nervous about that. Lynda picked out all my clothes. I don't know if I have any fashion sense. I certainly can't look at someone and have a good idea what size they wear like Lynda does."

"You'd do fine at the clothing store, but you'll shine at the gallery. You're too artistic for it not to be a good fit. I might even be able to help. I'm no artist, but I make some pretty good picture frames out of old wood."

"You made that one in the living room? The one framing the old picture of Colin Fraser on his horse?"

"I did. Made some for Caleb and Megan, and a couple for Lynda's house when the restoration is done. I put in a new corral last year. Parts of the old one had been here for at least fifty years. I used the wood for the frames, but there is a whole stack of it in the barn."

"Jake, those would be perfect for the Western scenes. Can you make some for the auction?"

"Sure. As long as I know what size prints you're going to use, I can go ahead and make them up. I have glass and a glass cutter out in the shop, and mat material and a cutter in my office."

"Whoo-hoo! This is going to be so cool!" She held up her hand for a high five.

Grinning, Jake lightly slapped her hand. "Yes, it is."

Seeing her excited, happy and full of purpose was the best part of it all.

CHAPTER TWELVE

Jake left about eight-thirty the next morning with the stock trailer. One of his Angus bulls had gone visiting on the Rocking K. Since he also had to repair the fence, he and Sunni decided to wait a day for her to go take more pictures. He left Licorice at the house to keep her company.

Lynda was still bubbling with plans for the gallery. Though her excitement was contagious, Sunni wanted more time before she committed to the project. "I don't know how I fell asleep so fast last night, but I didn't really have a chance to think it through carefully or pray about it. Let me mull it over today, and I'll give you an answer tonight."

"That's fine, hon. Don't pay me any mind. When I have an idea, especially if I think it's brilliant," she said with a grin, "I get as excited as a goat in a pepper patch. Now, I have to run. Talk to you tonight." She flew out the door, putting on a big gold hoop earring as she went.

A few minutes later, Sunni and Licorice walked out to the orchard. A cool breeze kept the temperature pleasant and filled the air with the fragrance of ripening peaches and plums. The peaches were still a tiny bit green but there were more than enough plums to fill the large bowl that she'd brought.

Birds were eating fruit that had fallen on the ground. Licorice scattered them, then took off after a squirrel while she picked the ripe plums from the tree. Before she'd filled the bowl halfway, he came back and stretched out in the shade to watch her work.

"Lord, I'd sure appreciate some clear direction about the gallery. You know I'd much rather work there than in a clothing store. Though I suspect we'd have more customers shopping for new pants and shirts than we will people in need of art-work. If we set up the online store, we might do all right. I need to know that I'm not charging off on my own in this, that You're in it with me."

She filled the bowl with plums, ate a couple and sat down on the bench in the orchard. Thinking about when she'd been there with Jake on Monday evening prompted a wistful sigh. He'd thought about kissing her. The longing she had seen in his eyes had mirrored her own. She'd wanted so much to reach up and pull his head down to hers.

"God, please help Jake and me hold to what is right. It's so difficult, Lord. He means so much to me already, and I've only known him a couple of weeks. I know he cares for me, too. I don't know what You want to teach us, except maybe to be obedient. We're both trying to do it.

"I'm confused. I love the man in my memories, my dreams. I don't know who he is, but the feelings I have for him run deep. But I care so much for Jake. I can't deny it. I'm falling in love with him, too. But how can I love two men at the same time? What will I do if I already have a husband? When my memory returns, how will I be able to have the same relationship with him, given what I feel for Jake? And why isn't he looking for me? Is he off in the wilds of the Amazon or something?"

Sunni paused. Though not common, it was a plausible reason for a man not to be searching for his missing wife. Was it just a figure of speech? Or was her subconscious trying to tell her something? She glanced at

Licorice, who watched her with his head tilted to one side.

"What do you think, boy?" The dog gave a little snort and laid his head down on his paws, closing his eyes. "You're no help. Come on. Let's go dig through Jake's cookbooks and see if I can find something to make with these plums. The Lord and I can have a discussion in the house as well as out here."

She found a recipe for plum kuchen that sounded good and was easy to make with ingredients they had on hand. Noting the time, she decided to save the cooking until after her weekly phone call with Dr. Smith.

Stretching out in Jake's recliner, which she had dubbed the long-distance version of a psychiatrist's couch, Sunni set the cordless phone on her lap. It rang two minutes later, the doctor being punctual as usual.

They quickly dispensed with the civilities and got down to business. She told the doctor about the photos and Lynda's idea to open a gallery. She also shared the memories she'd had since their last talk, specifically the one about the blond-haired man.

"Do you think he's the man in your dream? The one who has been shot?" asked the doctor.

"Maybe. I've never seen his face in the

dream, but based on the strength of my emotional reaction, I think it's likely. I know that I love him. But if I have a husband or boyfriend, I keep wondering why he hasn't reported me missing."

"That's a valid question," said the psychiatrist. "Perhaps he's out of the country, in some remote area where he can't contact you and doesn't realize you aren't where you're supposed to be."

Sunni stifled a gasp. "I was wondering a few minutes ago if he was in the wilds of the Amazon."

"Did something specific bring that to mind? One of your snippets of memory?"

"No. I was just talking to God. Ranting a little actually."

"It's certainly a possibility, as are several others. The two of you may have been having some difficulties and are separated, taking a break from each other and not having any contact for a while. Or the man you remember is part of your past."

"You think he's dead?" The mere suggestion brought pain.

"Given the anguish you feel when you have the dream, there's certainly a risk. He could have survived and you are simply reliving the horror of that night. You may have broken up, or if you were married, are now divorced. You should prepare yourself for the possibility that he's no longer a part of your life, Sunni," she said quietly. "For whatever reason."

"What if he is still part of my life?"

"Then you'll be prepared for the worst but receive the best."

How could it be the best when her heart would be torn between two men?

"Sunni?"

"I'm here."

"What are you thinking?"

"That this is confusing, that I'm a mess."

"You're doing quite well." The doctor paused, and Sunni thought she heard her tapping a pen against the desk. Doing her analyzing bit. Trying to pick her brain from two hundred miles away. "How's Jake?"

"He's good." Wonderful.

"How are you two getting along?"

"Peachy keen." Sunni rolled her eyes. What a stupid thing to say. She'd spent too much time in the orchard earlier.

But the doctor laughed. "I haven't heard that one in a while." She was quiet for a minute. "Did I make a mistake leaving you there?"

"No. Everyone here has been very supportive and kind."

"Especially Jake?"

"Yes."

"Are you falling for him?"

"Yes." Sunni swallowed hard. She didn't think he would be too happy if he knew she talked about him to the doctor. But she needed advice from someone who could be objective. "And he's falling for me. I'm concerned that when my memory returns, I'll discover I'm married or already involved with someone. I think he's worried about it, too."

"And you'd have to choose between them."

"I would honor the sanctity of marriage and go with my husband. Jake knows that. If I'm not married but in a relationship with someone, then I'd have to choose. It might be difficult."

"And not something to be done quickly or lightly. From what I've seen, and what Doc Hampton tells me, Jake is a fine man. In your circumstances, however, you're very vulnerable. When life returns to normal, your feelings for him may not be as intense or as deep as they seem right now. His may not be, either."

Another pause, more pencil tapping. Sunni wondered if the doctor realized she could hear it over the phone. Probably not.

"Are you sleeping with him?"

"No." Sunni wasn't surprised at the question. She might not remember her own history, but she knew that many people didn't think twice about hopping into bed with total strangers. The doctor probably dealt with that sort of thing all the time. "Nor is he pressuring me. We share the belief that it's wrong."

"It seems as if you're keeping things in perspective and under control. You've set boundaries and are staying within them. If I thought it would help you, I'd bring you up here to Lubbock, but I believe you'd be miserable. There are risks if your relationship with Jake deepens, but at this point, I think the benefits of you being there with him and his aunt and the friends you've made outweigh potential problems.

"I recommend taking the job at the gallery if Lynda goes ahead with it. And definitely keep taking pictures. Your enthusiasm for photography and the gallery is a good thing, Sunni. I believe it's a link to your past, and one you should explore as much as possible. When is the church potluck and auction?"

"A week from Saturday."

"I'll plan on attending it. I'd like to see you again in person, and I'd love to take a look at your pictures. I might even bid on some at the auction. I need more art for my office."

"I'll give you any prints you like." After she earned enough money to pay for them. "It won't even come close to what I should be paying you. Jake makes some great frames out of old corral wood if that's something you care for."

"I'll check them out. My office decor is a bit eclectic so they might work. Stay within the limits you've set for yourself, Sunni, but relax and enjoy the life you have now."

"Because I might not ever remember what I had before?"

"That's always a possibility, though I still think you'll get your memory back. Do you have *The Message Bible*?

"I think Lynda has one."

"Good. Look up Matthew 6:34 in it and you'll understand what I mean. Now, be sure and call if you need to. I'll see you a week from Saturday. Can you schedule a little private time together early Sunday afternoon?"

"Certainly." Sunni chuckled, feeling better after talking to her. "It's not like my calendar is all that full."

"Well, pencil me in anyway."

As soon as she hung up the phone, Sunni went into Lynda's room. She found *The*

Message Bible on a bookshelf next to the small lady's desk in front of the window.

Opening it to Matthew 6:34, she read, "Give your entire attention to what God is doing right now, and don't get worked up about what may or may not happen tomorrow. God will help you deal with whatever hard things come up when the time comes."

Sunni closed the Bible and placed it back on the shelf. "Thank You, Lord, for answering my prayer, for giving me Your clear direction. Thank You for what You're doing in my life right now. Thank You for Jake, the friends You've given me, photography and the opportunity to work. I'm not going to worry about the future. I give it all to You — my life, my work and my relationship with Jake. We're in Your hands, Lord. Guide us day by day on the path You've laid out for us. In Jesus' name, amen."

Humming a chorus they'd sung on Sunday and with God's peace filling her heart, she went into the kitchen and tried her hand at baking.

Later, when Jake ate half of the plum kuchen for lunch, she decided she could add baking to her list of talents.

Sunday morning, Jake was nervous as they

pulled into the church parking lot. It was worse than going to a church for the first time. Folks he didn't know would ask about him. What would the old-timers tell them?

He'd taken extra care as he dressed, quickly ruling out the slacks in his closet. He opted for his best black jeans and an almost-new shirt of charcoal-gray with light gray vertical stripes. Only as he shut off the engine did the aptness of his choice hit him. He was the black sheep returning to the fold. Would they really welcome him? Or receive him with coolness and whisper when he turned his back? Ron had assured him that all would be well. He prayed that his friend was right.

Jake caught Sunni watching him as they climbed out of the truck. Lynda dashed on ahead, anxious to talk to a neighbor whose cousin was a watercolor artist. She wanted to put some of his work in her gallery.

Sunni walked around the front of the pickup, stopping by the left fender as he closed his door. She wore a rose top in a crinkly cotton and a flowered skirt of various shades of rose and pink. Lynda had brought them out from the store the day before, along with a necklace and earrings to match. He wanted to stay right where they were so he could stare at her all day.

"You're movin' mighty slow, cowboy."

He grinned at her exaggerated Texas twang. "This is my normal speed. Unlike my aunt, I don't race through life at ninety miles an hour," he said as they walked toward the building.

"She is a bundle of energy. Especially since she started working on the gallery. I'm out of breath half the time from trying to keep up with her."

"She's all charged up and raring to go. I don't think I've ever seen her this excited or happy."

A rancher who lived about five miles down the road went up the church steps in front of them. On the porch, the man turned and shook hands with him.

"Good to see you, Jake." He nodded to Sunni. "Good mornin', Miss Sunni. How are you today?"

"Just fine, Ralph. Did your daughter have that grandbaby yet?"

"No, but anytime now." He patted the cell phone clipped to his belt. "I've got my phone on stun in case my son-in-law calls during the service. If you see me and the missus hightailing it out of here, you'll know why."

Jake suddenly realized how out of touch he had been with his neighbors. Lynda had mentioned that Ralph and Irene Crowley were going to be grandparents for the first time. She did her best to keep him up to speed on the local news that was worth repeating. He hadn't been paying enough attention to remember the details. Ralph had twin daughters, Patti and Maddi, and they were both married. He didn't have a clue which one was expecting.

"Do they know whether it's a boy or a girl?" He stepped back, nodding to another couple he didn't know as they went inside.

"A little boy. Patti said they're going to name him John Michael."

Jake hid a grin. All those years of prying information out of suspects paid off one more time.

"John is my middle name and Michael is Eric's dad's name. Makes a good combination." He turned toward the door. "Better get inside before Irene comes looking for me."

Jake shook hands with the greeter at the door, elderly Mr. McIntyre, who had been his Sunday school teacher when he was in junior high. The man beamed as he handed him a bulletin. "You back for good, son?"

"Yes, sir."

"Praise the Lord. Reckon I can quit prayin' for you every day now."

Quick moisture stung Jake's eyes, but he blinked it away. "I don't suppose I need them every day, but every once in a while might be a good idea."

The old man grinned. "I'll put you on my remember-now-and-then list. You can do the same for me."

"I'll do that."

The man turned a Jesus-filled smile on Sunni. "How are you today, little lady?"

"Very well, thank you. And you?" She smiled at him, exchanging pleasantries, then nodded at Lynda as she motioned for Sunni to join her. "I'd better see what Lynda wants. I'll catch up with you in a minute."

As she walked away, Mr. McIntyre touched Jake's arm, his expression filled with concern. "Has she recovered her memory?"

"No. She's remembered a few more things this week, but nothing that helps much. I'd appreciate it if you could keep her on your everyday prayer list."

"I will." The old man's gaze rested on Sunni. "She may not know who she is in a lot of ways, but she's a child of the King. Christ's love shines through her like a beacon on a dark night."

"Yes, it does." Jake leaned closer to his old

friend. "She's not afraid to set you straight either."

Mr. McIntyre laughed. "Pointed you in the right direction, did she?"

"Yes, sir. Herded me down the chute right into the arms of Jesus."

"No better place to be." He patted Jake on the back, then turned to another family coming up the steps.

The rest of the service went much the same. They shared a pew with Lynda, Toby, Caleb, Megan and the boys. If anyone thought Jake shouldn't be there, they hid it well. He lost count of how many folks made a point to say hello and let him know subtly — and sometimes not so subtly — that they were glad he was back.

Ron's preaching was as in-depth and thoughtful as ever. Jake had half expected him to teach on the prodigal son's return, but evidently the minister didn't think anyone there needed to be reminded of forgiveness and reconciliation on this particular Sunday.

Jake remembered most of the songs, though there were a few choruses that he'd never heard before. He was pleased to discover how well Sunni could sing. Her clear, sweet soprano blended perfectly with his baritone. The people in front of them even commented on how good they sounded together.

He noted a few speculative glances in their direction, but they weren't malicious. *Matchmaking* was the word that came to mind. Sitting next to Sunni, he resisted the urge to reach over and take her hand. Given that she was staying at his house, even with Lynda there, it wouldn't take much for people to jump to the wrong conclusions.

Halfway into the sermon, Jake finally relaxed and let the peace and joy of being with other believers and worshipping the Lord seep into his soul.

Thank You, God, for mercy and grace.

CHAPTER THIRTEEN

On Tuesday morning, Jake and Sunni carried the frames he had made into the kitchen and mounted the three art prints she was donating to the auction. She'd chosen the one of him and Caz in silhouette, an old windmill and adjacent stone water tank, and a breathtaking sunset over a mesa. They'd spent a couple of days the week before riding around the area in search of scenic shots. She'd taken a dozen photos and made notes on five other places where she wanted to use a tripod to hold the camera.

Along the way, Jake had swiped the camera and taken pictures of her. She'd been embarrassed at first and clowned around, but when he suggested that she play with Licorice, he'd gotten some good shots. Later he took some close-ups as she watched a hawk soar overhead, and a great one when she looked right at the camera and smiled just for him.

They propped the pictures up on the mantel above the fireplace and stood back to admire their handiwork. Jake gave her a one-armed hug. "We done good."

She laughed, slipping her arm around his waist, giving him a little squeeze. "Your frames and mats are perfect with the photos." Resting her head against his shoulder, she added softly, "We make a good team."

"Yes, we do," he murmured, laying his cheek against her hair, wishing their partnership could extend to every part of their lives. They quietly stood there for a few minutes, and Jake wondered if she were analyzing the pictures all over again. He leaned his head forward a tiny bit and peeked down at her. Her eyes were closed. A tiny frown wrinkled her brow and intense longing filled her face.

If he didn't move away within the next two seconds, he'd be kissing her silly. Hugging her a little tighter for one of those seconds, he prayed for strength and released her. When she opened her eyes and lifted her head from his shoulder, he stepped away, heading for the kitchen. "Are you still planning on helping Lynda today?"

"Yes." She strolled into the kitchen and began picking up the scraps of matting material. "She's getting her hair cut right now, then we're going to do some more cleaning at the gallery. We stripped off the old wallpaper, but there's a lot of dirt to take care of before we can paint."

"Do you need me to run you into town?"

"If you have time. If not, she'll come get me. She said she'd call when she's done at the beauty shop."

"I can take you." He smiled, feeling safer with the table between them. "You might talk me into buying you lunch at the Sonic."

"Somehow I don't think I'd have to talk very hard."

"Well, Licorice is mighty fond of their burgers."

She laughed, throwing the unusable pieces of matting in the garbage. "So is his side-kick." When Licorice trotted over to see what she was doing, she scratched his back and looked up at Jake. "Both sidekicks. This time get yourself a large order of fries so you don't steal mine."

"But fighting over yours is half the fun."

"Then I'll get onion rings." She straightened and blew a breath in his general direction. "That'll keep you at a safe distance."

Jake slowly shook his head. "They're as good as fries." An image of them both nibbling on the same onion ring popped into his head. He retrieved the mat cutter from

236

the table and practically ran down the hall to his office. When a man pictured an onion ring leading to a kiss, he was in big trouble.

He wound up staying in town helping with the cleanup. The gallery building had been built in 1910 and had been empty for about five years. The first thing Lynda had done was have the place fumigated, so the various critters that had taken up residence were no longer a problem. Sunni still made a face and shuddered every time she ran into a cobweb.

Though the wooden building had been closed up, more than a little dirt from West Texas sandstorms had blown through the cracks. Jake brought along his shop vacuum, which came in especially handy when tackling the dirt in the corners. He surveyed several cracks around the door and window frames. Sunlight filtered through them. Not a good sign. The inside wall was made of rough wood planks, a few of them too warped to nail down securely.

"The inspector didn't find any dry rot or termites?" He tapped a warped board with a hammer from the toolbox he kept in the truck.

"No." Lynda stopped sweeping and wiped her forehead with the back of her hand. Despite having the air-conditioning running full blast, they were all working up a sweat. "He said all the wood was sound, though some was warped and boards were loose in a few places, both inside and out. Using rough wood for the inside of that wall gives it a certain charm, but there's no insulation in it."

"No wonder the air conditioner is working so hard. All these cracks aren't helping any, either." Jake studied the side walls. One was covered in Sheetrock. The other was brick. Both also formed the walls of the adjoining buildings. "How fond are you of the old-wood look?"

"I like it, but I like keeping out the dust and heat or cold better."

"Will the owner pay for any renovations?" The building had been inherited a few years earlier by a man who lived in Memphis.

"No. He paid for the inspection and had a couple of minor wiring problems repaired to bring it up to code, but he said anything else I want to do will be on my dime."

"I think you should replace the outside trim around the door and windows after I fill the gaps with caulking. If we tear out these inside boards and put in some good insulation and Sheetrock, you'll save money in the long run."

"I was thinking that, too. I'll talk to the

carpenters who are working on my house, see if they'll take care of this first."

"I can take care of everything but mudding and taping the Sheetrock. Never have mastered that chore, so you'll need a professional."

"You have a ranch to run." Lynda walked over to examine the wall. She glanced back at Sunni, who was working at the rear of the store. "Although you don't seem to be spending too much time working there these days," she said, her eyes twinkling.

"Caught me at a good time. There's enough grass so I don't have to worry much about supplemental feeding. I check on the cattle every day, make sure they're all still there and none are sick or hurt. Except for repairing a broken fence and keeping the windmill operational, I can put off other projects for a few more weeks and help y'all get this place whipped into shape. Actually, I'd enjoy it." His attention drifted to Sunni.

"I'm sure you would." Lynda laughed quietly.

"Hey, it's fun to rip things apart and put up something new." He smiled at his aunt, knowing she saw right through to his ulterior motive — spending more time with the pretty blonde sweeping the back half of the store.

She looked cute dressed in an old T-shirt with a faded orca whale on the front and an old pair of Megan's jeans with the hems rolled up into a big cuff. He'd gotten the shirt at Sea World years ago. Her ponytail swayed along with the rest of her as she moved the broom to the beat of a lively Brooks & Dunn song on the radio. Licorice was stretched out nearby, watching her with adoration. "Besides, I gotta keep my dog happy."

His aunt grinned, resting her hand on his back. "That dog sure has taken up with her."

"If she's around, he picks her company over mine more often than not. If he didn't like to ride in the pickup so much, he'd probably never hang out with me." It wasn't quite true but close. Licorice obviously loved her. And who could blame him?

"All right, nephew, I'll let you play contractor and construction crew. I don't want to stand in the way of you having fun." Lynda grinned and went back to sweeping.

Whistling along with a new song on the radio, Jake strolled out to the truck and dug the pry bar out of the toolbox. If anybody had told him a month earlier that he'd be helping renovate a building in town and actually enjoying it, he would have told them they weren't playing with a full deck.

■ ■ ■ ■

They spent the rest of the week working on the gallery, laughing, joking and having a good time despite the hard, dirty work. They took sandwiches for lunch but indulged in takeout for supper every night — barbecue, tacos, fried catfish and pizza with the works. By Friday night, they had the place ready for the Sheetrock to be mudded and taped on Monday.

"So, boss lady, do we get the weekend off?" Jake groaned a little as he leaned back in the recliner.

"Yes, we do." Lynda winced as she settled in the rocker and put up her feet. "At least from working at the gallery. Tomorrow Sunni and I have to prepare a few dishes for the potluck. I suppose you need to do a few things around here."

"Just the normal drive around the ranch to check on things. Otherwise, Lic and I plan to be real lazy. What are you taking to the potluck?"

"A big bowl of fruit salad — watermelon, cantaloupe, nectarines, strawberries and anything else I decide to throw in. And a mess of black-eyed peas. I still have some frozen from my garden last year."

"Not that I know what they taste like, but why would you make a mess of them?" Sunni stretched out on the couch with a yawn.

"That's just one of our sayings. Come to think of it, I don't know why we call it a mess of peas. Nor can I describe what they taste like. But the ones we put up in the freezer fresh from the garden sure don't taste like the canned, frozen or dried ones you buy in a grocery store. I'll give you a sample in the morning."

"Okay." Sunni yawned again, triggering one from Jake and then Lynda.

"We're a real lively bunch." Jake met Sunni's sleepy gaze. "No partyin' tonight."

"I hope I'm not this tired tomorrow." She tucked another orange pillow beneath her head.

"Or this sore." Jake shifted in the chair, trying to ease an ache in his shoulder. "I used muscles I forgot I had. When I put that last screw in the Sheetrock, I was happy as a hog in slop."

Sunni giggled and clamped her hand over her mouth. Then she giggled again.

"What's so funny?" Smiling, Jake watched her trying to control her laughter.

"A hog in slop." She let out a whoop. "Imagining you with pointed ears and a big snout." She laughed until tears ran down her cheeks.

"Did I snort?" He wiggled his nose. When she nodded and burst into more giggles, Jake smiled indulgently and shook his head. "I know somebody who's worn out."

"Got the sillies," said Lynda.

"Is that what you call it?" Jake chuckled when Sunni whooped again.

"You'd better carry that girl off to bed."

Jake raised an eyebrow. "Auntie, I do believe you get a little rowdy when you're tired."

Lynda grinned mischievously. "Just dump her on the bed and leave, nephew. Walk out and close the door."

Jake stood slowly. "She does look too tired to walk down the hall."

Sunni stopped giggling and stared at him, her eyes wide. Wiping her cheeks, she sat up with a hiccup and swung her legs down to the floor. "Uh, I can walk okay."

"Oh, I don't think so." Jake glanced at his aunt and winked, then almost choked when she smirked. She was supposed to be playing chaperon, not Cupid.

He walked over to the couch and held out his hand. Sunni hesitated, then took hold of it, and he pulled her up to stand. Before she had a chance to protest again, he swept her up in his arms.

She blinked, wrapped her arms around his neck and smiled nervously. "Don't you dare dump me on the bed, Jake Trayner."

"You can pretend it's a trampoline. That's what my cousins and I used to do when they came to visit."

"It'll ruin the mattress." She attempted to look prim, but a smile won out. "And I might bounce off and hurt myself."

He carried her down the hall. "Can't have that, can we?"

"No." The words came out a little breathless as he stopped in front of her door.

"The carriage stops here."

"Not a bad pun."

He slowly lowered her feet to the floor, then caressed her jaw with his thumb. "I don't think we should let Lynda get this tired again."

Sunni smiled, her eyes sparkling. "She does become mischievous."

"Stirring up trouble is more like it."

"As if we needed somebody shoving us toward each other."

Jake chuckled and lowered his hand. "We're accomplishing that pretty well on our own. Good night, Sunni."

"Good night, Jake. I'll see you in the morning."

He nodded and started to turn away, but she put her hand on his arm, stopping him. When he looked back at her, she quickly stood on tiptoe and brushed a kiss on his cheek. Then she spun around and hurried into her room, shutting the door without looking at him.

Of such things dreams were made.

CHAPTER FOURTEEN

Sunni stared at the three long tables filled with at least a dozen casseroles, two heaping platters of fried chicken, another of tamales, two bowls of black-eyed peas, one of pinto beans, some weird-looking stuff that Jake said was fried okra, a dozen or more salads and easily a dozen cakes, pies or plates of cookies. "Even if I took only a teaspoonful, I can't possibly try everything."

"That's the trouble with potlucks. Have to make tough decisions." Jake grabbed a tamale and a spoonful of pinto beans. "Looks like these ladies are still good cooks. You should try a little of the okra. It's one of those things that you either love or hate. I happen to like it." He added a little bit to his plate. "I already see that I'll have to come back for seconds."

Sunni took a tamale, then a little of this and a little of that from the casserole section. Definitely a spoonful of Lynda's black-eyed peas. She'd tried some at the house earlier, and they were delicious. A few chunks of watermelon, small spoonfuls of several salads and her plate was full. "Look at those desserts. Can we take something for later in the afternoon? I'll be too full after I eat this."

"Don't see why not. We can stow the plates in the cooler. Let's come back when we finish off this. There should be enough desserts left to find something good."

The little church didn't have a fellowship hall. Even if the pews had been removable, there wouldn't have been room inside for everyone. The crowd was about twice as big as the group who attended on Sunday. Sunni smiled at Waylon, the photographer, who walked by with his niece and family.

She and Jake walked over to their lawn chairs under one of the cloth awnings set up for the occasion. Toby and Lynda joined them, as did Doc Hampton and his wife, Beth, and Dr. Smith who told them to call her Roberta. Caleb, Megan and the kids came along a few minutes later, with Cody plopping down on the grass next to Sunni's chair. He looked up at her and grinned, then dug into his food as only a hungry boy could do.

"Where did all these people come from?"

Sunni unwrapped the corn husk from the tamale, dropping the husk on the ground next to Jake's. They would pick them up after they were done.

"The kids did a great job of selling tickets." Doc speared a chunk of melon. "Even though we attend church in town, coming to this potluck is a tradition for us." He nodded toward his wife. "Beth grew up on the Davis Ranch south of here."

"It's always been as much of a community get-together as one for the church folks." Jake took a drink of soda.

"We have a lot of friends who live out this way," said Doc. "Gives us a chance to visit. I don't have time for that at the office."

"And they always have the best things for the auction," said Beth. "Thelma's quilts are always a hit, as is the afghan Bonnie makes every year."

"This year, they have Sunni's photographs to liven up the action, too." Doc smiled at her. "I'm aiming to bid on the one of Jake and his horse. It will look great in my office."

"Better in our family room at home." His wife winked at him and grinned at Sunni. "I can see a friendly argument brewing already."

"I'll resolve that issue before it starts

because I'm getting that one for my office in Lubbock." Roberta wagged her fork at her old friends. "And don't you dare outbid me for it."

"I'll give you both a copy for free," Sunni said quietly. "I owe you more than I can repay for your good care."

"That's real sweet of you," said Doc. "But don't forget that the whole idea here is to raise money for the mission trip. Tell you what, if we don't manage to snag it, have another print made up. We'll pay the going price and donate it to the kids for the trip."

"Same goes for me." Roberta glanced around at the crowd. "I expect the bidding will go high on it."

"I want the sunset picture," said Toby. "God's glory and God's country all rolled into one."

"Oh, I like that." Lynda gave him a hundred-watt smile. "Sunni, that's what we should call it for the gallery. God's Glory, God's Country."

"How many will you have in the gallery, Sunni?" Beth shooed a fly away from her plate.

"The three here, plus some others."

"As many as she can do." Lynda waved her fork in the air as she spoke. "The fine-art prints will be signed and limited edition.

No more than one hundred of each. We'll have a framed one on display with a few others in frames stashed in the store room." She made a face and chuckled. "Oh, dear, that sounds like we shipped them in from China. Anyway, we'll mount a few in frames and some just in mats in case people want a different kind of frame. The others we'll store in special acid-free boxes and use as needed.

"We'll also do them up as lithographs. Those aren't as good a quality, so we can sell them a lot cheaper. I'm looking into having note cards made, too."

"Are you going to sell them over the Internet?" asked Roberta.

"Yes. We've been checking into it in our spare time. As in at night, if we can stay awake past supper. Needless to say, we haven't gotten a lot done on it yet. We're concentrating on opening the gallery first, then we'll dive into the Internet operation with all four feet."

To Sunni's relief, the conversation moved on to other topics, all of them lively and fun. She contributed at times but generally found herself growing more and more quiet — and nervous. She would be thankful for whatever amount her prints brought for the fund-raiser, but she feared that Lynda's expectations were too high. Several of the things being auctioned off were just as nice or much better than her prints.

After they ate, she and Jake wandered into the church building to take another look at the things that had been donated. There were so many contributions that only a limited number would actually be sold by the auctioneer. The rest were displayed on tables set around three sides of the sanctuary for purchase through a silent auction. Everyone had received a number when they arrived at the potluck. In front of each item was a bidding sheet. If a person wanted the item, they entered their number and the amount of the bid on the sheet. The final bid would be the winner.

The assortment of donations provided something for just about anyone. Homemade jams and pickles; silk flower arrangements; an antique purse; a pie a month, buyer's choice of kinds; toys, some store-bought, some handmade. Baskets of goodies, a crocheted baby blanket, an offer to plow a field, ten bales of alfalfa hay, clover honey, one free day of working a roundup, crystal vases, matching earrings and necklace, an expensive Stetson felt hat in the winner's size donated by an out-of-town Western-wear store, and a home-cooked meal by one of the single ladies.

Jake chuckled as he read the long bidding list on the home-cooked dinner. "Looks like a couple of people are in a bidding war for Angie's dinner."

"Bachelors, I assume?" Without thinking, Sunni leaned against his arm as she read the list.

"No doubt. Whoa, somebody else tagged on a bid here at the end." He whistled softly. "Seventy-five dollars. That guy really has his eye on the lady. That's a big jump from the previous bid of forty."

Realizing that there wasn't a breath of air between them, Sunni edged away about six inches. "Somebody is making a statement."

Jake glanced at her, wishing she'd stayed pressed against him. It might not have been smart if they wanted to keep people from talking, but it sure was nice. "Good for him. Angie was in my class in school. She became a teacher and lived in East Texas for a while. She came home ten years ago to care for her sick mama. Knowing Angie, she did it lovingly, without complaint. Now that her mother has passed, it's time for her to have a life of her own."

"I think at least one gentleman agrees with her."

"So it seems." They moved on to the next

table. "Now, this I like." Jake picked up a hand-tooled leather belt. The sign said the purchaser could have any name of his choosing added at no charge. He held it around his waist. "Right size. I think I'll bid on this. The last bid is twenty dollars. I'll up it five and see where it goes from there." He jotted down the bid and his number on the sheet and moved on.

When they reached the items that would be auctioned in open bidding, Sunni stopped to admire the handmade pieced quilt in a multicolored log-cabin pattern. "Now that's a work of art. Look at those perfect, tiny stitches. The fabric looks vintage, or at least it's a reproduction of vintage fabric. I can't imagine how long it took to make this."

She had high praise for the afghan, too, but Jake was more impressed with the pair of ornate silver spurs next to it. They would bring in a bundle. Not that he would be bidding on them. He didn't have a need for fancy spurs.

Caleb had donated a purebred Angus calf. He'd left the calf at home but her picture and pedigree were displayed on an easel. His reputation for honesty and the quality of his cattle were all anyone needed to buy the animal sight unseen.

When Sunni came to a necklace and breathed a soft "Oh," Jake knew he'd found what he wanted. The pendant was the outline of Texas in gold with a beautiful lavender freshwater pearl mounted slightly to the left of center. "That's a Concho pearl. The freshwater mussels, and consequently sometimes the pearls, are found here in West Texas along the Concho River and the south fork of the Colorado River. Also in various lakes those rivers feed into."

"Doesn't concho mean shell in Spanish?"

"That's right. Spanish explorers found the mussels along the river and gave it the name."

"It's beautiful. I've never seen a lavender pearl." She shrugged and smiled. "Well, I don't think I have. Sheesh, this no-memory stuff gets annoying."

Jake laughed, proud of her for not letting it get her down. "They're pretty rare. It matches your blouse."

"I hadn't noticed."

"Right." Jake grinned at her. "Seems to me that you have a couple of other tops that this would go with."

"I do but I'm fine with the cute necklaces that Lynda gave me."

He leaned down to murmur in her ear. "You should have something pretty, not cute. I'm going to bid on it."

"No, you don't need to do that."

"I know I don't need to. I want to."

"Jake, no."

"You want to fight about it?" They had drawn the attention of several people.

"No." Sunni glanced around and ducked her head, a flush coloring her face. "But you shouldn't spend any more money on me. Good grief, you're already paying for everything now."

Something I hope to do always. "I promise if the bidding goes crazy, I'll drop out." When she looked up at him, he barely kept himself from wiping away her frown with his fingertip.

He hurried on in a teasing tone as another couple reached the afghan. "So don't argue with me, woman." Resting his hand lightly in the small of her back, he guided her away from the items on display toward the door. "Besides, it's time I made a statement, too. In case any of these hombres start gettin' ideas about asking you out."

"They don't even know me."

"That doesn't mean anything. They like what they see so far. In case you haven't noticed, we're long on bachelors and short on single women around here."

She scanned the crowd as they stepped

outside. "I can't tell who is married and who isn't. Even most of the couples have split up, visiting with other people. Except us."

"Us a couple. I like the sound of that. So do you want to split up and go visit with the ladies while I join the guys?"

"No." Her answer was as quick as a hiccup and a little on the sharp side.

Jake figured he knew why. Every single man there, except for the two who were talking to Angie, had zeroed in on Sunni the minute she stepped out of the church. Quite a few married men were looking, too. He supposed just because a man was married didn't mean he couldn't admire a pretty woman. "Are you okay?"

"I don't like being the center of attention."

"Hard to avoid when you're the prettiest woman here." They walked down the steps and around to the back of the building where some of the kids were taking turns on the swing set. Farther over, others, including the Morrison boys, were playing baseball. Jake and Sunni stopped where they could watch the game but have a little space to themselves.

"What did you mean by making a statement?" she asked, keeping her face turned toward the kids.

"To let any man who lays eyes on you know that if he wants to ask you out, he has to go through me."

"Like some protective big brother?"

"Hardly." He slipped his arm around her waist, deciding he didn't care if somebody saw them. "Like a man protecting his woman." When she started to speak, he placed his finger lightly on her lips. "I know I don't have any right to make that claim, but that's how I feel, sugar. And I'm not about to let some smooth talker crowd me out before I have a chance with you."

"Gettin' all macho on me, cowboy?"

"Guess I am." He grinned. "Do you like it?"

She laughed and relaxed against his side. "Just don't take it too far. No fisticuffs."

He chuckled and tightened his arm. "I'm not planning on any. I'm not as young as I used to be. Maybe we should act like a couple for the rest of the day. Just to make sure the message gets across."

She looked up at him, a smile lighting her face. "Jake, we haven't been apart since we got here. I think most people already have that idea."

He released her and searched her eyes. "Does that bother you?"

She held his gaze and said firmly, "Not at all."

Lynda came around the corner. "There you are. Come on, you two, the auctioneer is about to begin." She grinned when Jake grabbed Sunni's hand, and they hurried toward her. "We've already moved the chairs so we can get settled before they start."

"Can't I hide around here until it's over?" asked Sunni.

"Nope." Lynda shifted to Sunni's side and hooked an arm through hers. "Can't miss all the fun."

"I'm not so sure it's going to be fun. What if nobody bids on the prints? Or they don't bring what you think they should?"

"Don't you worry about that, hon. I'll be happy with whatever they bring in, though I'm sure it's going to be good. People have been raving about them all afternoon. So you just relax and try to enjoy it."

Sunni knew she wouldn't relax until the whole thing was over, but she did her best not to let her nervousness show. Some of the men had carried the items to be auctioned off outside, setting them up in the shade of the building.

After everyone was seated, in chairs or on the ground, the high school group sang a couple of songs, one in English and one in

Spanish. Then they gave a brief overview of the orphanage in Mexico where they were going to work for a week helping add a one-room annex to the school. Their excitement and love for the children and the adults who worked at the orphanage eased some of her tension.

It's all for You, Jesus, and these precious children, both those who are going and those they will help. May my contribution serve in whatever way pleases You.

CHAPTER FIFTEEN

The auctioneer, Murphy Jones, was a local man who handled estate sales and auctions. The first item was a trip in a hot-air balloon for four people.

There was a lot of joking back and forth as a burly rancher and one of his employees kept upping the bid. The cowboy finally backed off, saying his boss didn't pay him enough to afford to go any higher, evoking boisterous laughter.

The rancher then turned around and invited the man and his wife to accompany "me and the missus as we fly through the air with the greatest of ease."

To which the cowboy replied, "We ain't tryin' out a blooming trapeze. But we'll come along on the ride anyway."

Next came Thelma's quilt. Murphy described the materials used and the number of hours the woman had spent on the project. Sunni quickly realized that the

people there were generous. Several partici-
pated in the bidding, with the final offer being five hundred dollars. Thelma was tickled
with the result, though Sunni thought it
might have sold for more at a store or online.

While most of the bidders on the quilt had
been women, the men jumped into the action hot and heavy for the silver spurs. One
of the younger cowboys, enjoying a brief
respite from the rodeo circuit, took them
home for three hundred dollars.

Then the auctioneer walked over to Sunni's photographs.

She took a deep breath and shifted closer
to Jake. He glanced down at her and put his
arm around her.

"Ladies and gentlemen, these three photographs were taken by Sunni, the young lady
staying with Jake and his aunt Lynda at
Fraser Creek Ranch. I expect most of you
know Sunni's story. If you're from out of
town and don't know about the woman who
has won our hearts, ask one of the locals to
tell you about her."

He checked the note card in his hand.
"These are *zhee-clay* fine-art prints." A soft
murmur went through the crowd. Sunni
noticed a couple of people nearby frowning
and checking the item list. "Now, the way

the word is spelled, seems like it should be *giclee.* But it's French and Waylon coached me on the proper way to say it. He also tells me this is the newest technology for reproducing photos or paintings into fine-art prints. They have even used it for some things in the Metropolitan Museum in New York, as well as numerous other museums and galleries.

"There is a description of the process on your sheets if you want more detail. These are done on the highest quality watercolor paper, using archival inks that have a life expectancy of over one hundred twenty-five years.

"Now, if the technical jargon makes your eyes glaze over, just remember that these are the finest large prints that can be made from a photo, and they'll likely last beyond your lifetime. Also keep in mind that these are limited edition. They may be used in other ways, such as lithographs, which aren't as nice, or note cards, etcetera, but there will never be more than one hundred of each printed in this fine-art format. These are signed, number one in each series.

"The whole process has been done locally, from Sunni taking the pictures to having them developed and printed by Waylon Cummings at his graphics shop in town.

The frames were made by Jake Trayner out of old corral wood."

Lynda hopped to her feet. "And if you miss out on these, you can pick one up at the gallery Sunni and I are opening in town."

"Can't beat that for helping the local economy," hollered Coyote Springs's mayor.

"That's right. But help out the kids first." With a big grin, Lynda sat back down amid smiles and chuckles.

Murphy waved his note card, drawing their attention back to him. "I've done a little checking — not with Lynda, but with an unbiased source — and found that art photos like these, this size, reproduced in the same way and framed, sell for three to four hundred dollars."

Sunni gasped softly. Lynda had mentioned the three-hundred-dollar figure, which she'd thought was high. But four hundred? For a well-known artist, maybe. Not an unknown. It suddenly occurred to her that if she truly was as good a photographer as everyone said — something she wasn't convinced of yet — did she already have a Web site? Was her identity out there waiting for her to discover? She felt kind of silly for not having thought of it before but blamed it on being so busy getting ready for the auction and the gallery opening.

"Why so thoughtful?" asked Jake.

"Do you suppose I already have a Web site to sell my photos under my real name?"

"I haven't found it."

"You've been looking?"

He nodded. "Several times after I saw those first pictures. If I have stumbled across it, I don't know it. A lot of Web sites don't have a picture of the photographer."

"Oh."

Jake glanced toward the makeshift stage in the shade of the church building. "Heads up, sugar, he's ready to open the bidding."

The auctioneer stood beside the silhouette of Jake and Caz. "I have a feeling that this is a picture of Jake Trayner. Hard to tell for certain, but given how close he's sitting to the photographer, it's probably a good guess." He got a good laugh from the crowd, and Sunni's face turned pink.

Jake didn't move an inch, for which she was grateful.

Murphy's expression sobered. "This picture is a symbol of every one of the ranchers and cowboys here and all those who aren't." He glanced around and cleared his throat. "It pays homage to our fathers, grandfathers, great-grandfathers, even great-great-grandfathers who settled this land and kept it for our generation and the ones to follow after us. Almost a hundred years ago, the world said the cowboy was a dying breed." He looked at Sunni. "Sunni, you've proved them wrong. And Lynda, if you're smart, you'll set the limit higher on this edition."

Longing welled up in Sunni's heart. No matter what happened between her and Jake, she hoped she could stay in this community, with these good people. *And stop running.* She caught her breath, wondering where that thought came from. But she didn't have a chance to dwell on it. The auction was starting. She closed her eyes, wanted to clamp her hands over her ears, too. "I can't look."

"Who'll open the bidding? Do I hear fifty?"

Sunni felt Jake move and heard the audience laugh. She peeked at him. Grinning, Jake waved his bidding card high in the air.

The auctioneer chuckled. "Jake, I don't think you're supposed to bid on your own stuff. You made the frame, remember?"

"But it's the best I've ever done." His expression was pure innocence.

She poked him in the ribs with her elbow.

"Oof!" He bent over slightly and grabbed his side. The crowd roared.

"Behave yourself," she scolded. Then she smiled. How could she not when he was so proud of himself? She knew exactly what he was up to — helping her to relax.

"Yes, ma'am." He straightened and gave her shoulder a slight squeeze.

"We have fifty, do I hear sixty?" Murphy nodded at Doc Hampton. "We have sixty, do I hear seventy-five? Seventy-five from bidder number twelve." Dr. Roberta Smith. "Do I hear one hundred? One hundred from bidder twenty-five." A middle-aged man Sunni didn't know. She thought he might be a rancher, but how did one tell? Most of these men dressed like cowboys whether or not they were.

And so it went at a nice, steady pace, with about eight people starting out and dwindling down to Doc, Roberta and the maybe-rancher until they'd reached four hundred dollars.

Heart pounding from sheer nerves, Sunni stretched up and whispered in Jake's ear. "Who is the other guy bidding on it?"

He leaned down, his breath whispering against her ear, making her shiver. "That's T. D. Martin. He owns a big ranch west of here on which he has about two hundred oil wells. He also owns a zillion shares in an oil company and who knows what else. He's

266

worth millions."

Sunni stared at him, mouthing, "Millions?"

Jake nodded and leaned down to her ear again. "And he just jumped the bid to six hundred dollars on *your* photo."

"No way." How could a whisper squeak? Scrunching her eyes shut, Sunni clamped her hand over one ear and buried the other against Jake's shoulder.

She could still hear the auctioneer.

"We have six hundred dollars. Do I hear six twenty-five? Six twenty-five? Going once at six hundred dollars. Going twice . . . sold to Mr. T. D. Martin for six hundred dollars."

Jake put both arms around her and squeezed the stuffing out of her. When he relaxed his hold and let her straighten, he was about to bust his buttons. "And you thought it might not bring in much."

Lynda danced a jig in front of her chair and almost knocked it over. Sunni didn't know if folks were clapping for Lynda or how much the photo brought.

"Oh, my." She was about to hyperventilate and fanned her face with the item sheet. "Oh, my."

Jake shoved her water bottle into her hand. "Drink."

She obeyed, listening in a daze as Murphy auctioned off the other two prints. She knew they wouldn't bring as much. They were good but didn't have the sentimental value that the cowboy one had. Still, several people bid on them. Roberta paid three hundred fifty dollars for the old windmill.

Privately, Sunni had insisted that they give Toby a copy of the sunset picture, which Lynda was more than happy to do. He still started off bidding on it, enjoying friendly rivalry and banter with Jake and a handful of others as they kept the bid moving upward. Jake and Toby dropped out about halfway. The print sold for three hundred to the chairman of the First Baptist Church in Coyote Springs, who intended to hang it in the church foyer.

Lost in thought, thanking the Lord for blessing her work and praying that He might be glorified through it, Sunni barely noticed when the afghan and Caleb's cute little calf were auctioned off.

When the auctioneer announced the last item, she felt Jake tense. Focusing on Murphy, she saw that he was ready to auction off the Concho pearl necklace. He gave a brief description of it, the history of the pearls and encouraged the men to step up and buy something pretty for their women-folk.

"Who'll start us off with fifty dollars?" A hand went up. "I see fifty. Do I hear sixty?"

"Two hundred dollars," called Jake. Sunni and half the audience gasped. She stared at him as people craned their necks to see who made the bid.

The auctioneer laughed. "You in a hurry, Jake?"

"Yes, sir. I'm ready to eat that piece of chocolate cake I have in my cooler."

Amid good-natured laughter, Murphy continued. "We have two hundred. Do I hear two twenty-five?" A hand went up three rows in front of them.

"Three hundred," called Jake.

"Jake!" Sunni didn't want him spending that much money on something for her. Even if it did warm her heart.

"You really are in a hurry," said Murphy.

"Got a piece of Miss Rose's lemon-chiffon pie in the cooler, too."

The people around them laughed and shook their heads. At least a dozen sent knowing glances in Sunni's direction.

"We have three hundred. Do I hear three twenty-five?" Murphy slowly scanned the audience. "No more takers? Jake's gonna look mighty funny wearing that necklace."

There were a few snickers, then somebody hollered, "He's got a different neck in mind to wear that trinket. Let the man have it."

Murphy grinned and winked at Sunni. "I think you pegged that one right, Sam. Three hundred going once. Three hundred going twice. Sold."

While Sunni chatted with Megan, Jake hurried over to pay. There was already a line at the table, so he had to wait about ten minutes. "I bid on the belt, too."

Pastor Ron's wife checked the bidding sheet and his number. "Missed out on that one."

Jake wrote his check and picked up the necklace. Tucking the box into his shirt pocket, he worked his way back through the crowd, shaking a few hands, receiving some teasing along the way.

He was anxious to leave and give her the necklace in private, but she was talking with T. D. Martin. When he stepped up beside her, he and Martin shook hands.

"Mr. Martin wants me to take some photos of his ranch." Excitement danced in Sunni's eyes as she looked up at Jake.

"Very limited edition prints," said the millionaire with a smile. "I figure about four copies of each. The wife and I have two other homes, one in Dallas and one in

Colorado. We enjoy spending time there but always get lonesome for the ranch. So do our two kids who are off at college. With Miss Sunni's photos, we'll have part of the ranch with us."

"That's great." Jake glanced at Sunni, uneasiness crawling down his spine. He was happy for her, but at the same time he wondered if he would lose her to this blossoming career. Once Martin's acquaintances saw her work, they'd be clamoring for some of their own. "Are you going to start on it soon?"

"Probably not for a few months, at least. I have to help Lynda get the gallery up and running first."

"Whenever she's ready," said Martin. "I understand about prior commitments and like it when people stick with them." A twinkle lit his eyes. "I'll let you two run along. You have better things to do than shoot the breeze with me. You have my card, ma'am. But if I don't hear from you in a couple of months, I'll give Trayner a call."

Jake flashed him a relieved smile. "Thanks." He grabbed her hand and tugged her toward the door. "Let's go home to eat the dessert." He heard Martin chuckle. It was nice to know the man wasn't impressed with his own self-importance and had a

sense of humor. Appearing slightly bemused, Sunni looked back over her shoulder
and gave Martin a little wave.

Jake had loaded his cooler in the truck
after they ate, so they only had to pick up
the lawn chairs. He accomplished that in
record time. Lynda and Toby were still visiting with friends. He caught her knowing
glance and figured she understood that he
wanted — really, really wanted — some
time alone with Sunni.

When they arrived back at the house, Jake
carried the cooler inside, setting it on the
kitchen counter. Licorice wandered in to
welcome them home. "Brought you some
nibbles, big guy. I saved a bit of chicken for
you."

"And I saved some vegetable salad." Sunni
scratched the dog behind the ear in his
favorite spot. "And a meatball."

"But you can wait a few minutes, mutt. I
have something to give Sunni first." Licorice
tipped his head to one side, looked from
one to the other, then lay down, watching
them intently.

Jake took the jewelry box from his pocket.
Opening it, he carefully took out the necklace. And suddenly felt clumsy. He'd never
given a woman anything like it.

"This is really sweet of you. But I still feel

guilty about you spending so much money."

"It went for a good cause. Two good causes, actually. See how the pearl is slightly offset to the left side of the state, so it's in West Texas? It's probably supposed to indicate San Angelo and the Concho Valley, but since it's an odd shape, it covers this area, too." He pointed to a spot near the top right edge of the pearl. "I figure that's my ranch right there."

Still examining the pendant, she smiled and nodded. "Works for me."

Silently asking the Lord to please let this be right, he moved behind her and fastened the chain around her neck. He rested his hands on her shoulders. "No matter where life takes you, this will be a reminder that you'll always have a home right here in the sweetest part of Texas — Fraser Creek Ranch." Lightly kissing her temple, he added in a whisper, "With me."

CHAPTER SIXTEEN

A week had passed since Jake had given her the necklace and whispered the words that filled her with soul-deep yearning. Other than the tiny caress on her temple, he hadn't kissed her. She didn't know if he had exerted restraint because he sensed things might get out of control or if he had hoped that she would kiss him in appreciation of the gift.

But in those moments, she hadn't dared. She longed for too much — to belong to him and to be loved by him, in every sense of the word.

The overwhelming love she felt for this man frightened her. Was it a love that could not be? One that would be wrong in man's eyes and forbidden in God's? She would never know, never be free while her memories were hidden, and her mind held her captive.

"How long must I wait, Lord? Please,

please end this. Open my eyes and my heart so I'll hurry up and learn what it is You're teaching me. Finish whatever work You're doing in me. I want to trust You, Lord. I want to believe that You brought us together, that the love we share is Your gift to us.

"But I know that people have free will and minds of our own. So there is a chance that You didn't plan on Jake and I falling in love. That You put me here for an entirely different reason, maybe to protect me somehow, so I'll stop running." She had no idea what she was running from, but it clearly seemed the thought she'd had during the auction was a clue to her past.

Picking up the necklace from the bedside table, she put it on as she did every morning, and traced her finger over the outline of the state, resting it on the pearl. "This is where I want to stay, God. Where my heart is."

Hearing Jake's footsteps in the hallway, she grabbed the box with her photos. When she opened the door, he had his hand raised, ready to knock.

"Good timing." His smile said he was glad to see her, even if they'd had breakfast together half an hour earlier. "Two more seconds and I might have rapped you on the forehead. I put the extra leaves in the dining room table. It's all ready for you and Lynda to lay out your pictures and decide how to use them."

"I'd like your suggestions, too." She stepped into the hallway as he moved aside.

"I don't know if I'd be much help. I like them all. But if you leave something out that I think should be included, I'll let you know later." He peeked out the front window. "Here comes Caleb. If I don't hustle out to meet him, he'll give me a bad time about making him late for the cattle auction. He doesn't really need my opinion about the stock, but we haven't done anything together for a while."

Not since she'd been there, at least not just the two of them. "He's probably feeling neglected."

Jake looked at her thoughtfully. "Could be. He's not exactly a party animal. Other than Megan and the kids, I'm about the only one he hangs out with. See y'all this afternoon."

He went out the front door, and Lynda came in the back. "What a lovely morning. I decided to have another cup of coffee and sit on the porch for a while. Are you ready to get started?"

"I'm ready."

They worked all morning, sorting photos and making lists of which ones would be done as fine-art prints, lithographs or both. Then they tried to narrow those down to the eleven to use first, in addition to the three they'd sold at the auction.

Jake had made five frames but was waiting on the rest until they decided what size they wanted. They were also considering having a few different frames made at a shop in San Angelo to test the market.

The picture-hanging hardware for the gallery had arrived the day before. Lynda planned to have her carpenters install it on Monday since they were waiting on delivery of some doors and window frames for her house. If things went according to plan, they'd be open in plenty of time for Trade Days.

By mid-afternoon, they'd finished all they could do. Lynda sat down in her rocking chair to read a book and promptly dozed off. Sunni made a meatloaf and put it in the refrigerator so it would be ready to cook for dinner. Then she read all ten pages of the local newspaper and a couple of chapters of Galatians.

When Caleb and Jake drove up, she and Licorice strolled out to meet them. She left Lic to greet Jake and walked around to the driver's side. "I don't see any cows in your trailer."

"They were all too scrawny." Caleb rested his arm in the open window. "Or else I'm too cheap."

Jake climbed out the passenger's side. "Too cheap to buy cattle. He did buy my lunch."

"Generous of me, too. If you haven't figured it out yet, that boy can eat."

Sunni laughed and looked over the hood at Jake. "Did you save any nibbles for Licorice?"

"Nope. If you don't tell him, he won't know the difference. Hey, dog. What are you doing?"

"He probably smells that ketchup you spilled on your jeans." Caleb grinned at Sunni. "He needs a big bib that reaches his knees."

Jake laughed and gently shoved Licorice away. "That's exactly what he found. Come on, boy, I think you need somebody to play with you." He waved at Caleb and touched Licorice on the back. "Tag, you're it." Jake trotted around the yard with Licorice chasing him. The dog caught up with him, nudging him in the leg with his nose.

"Now you're it, Jake." Laughing, Caleb turned back to Sunni. "I'd better boogie. If you head on to the porch first, you might not get covered with dust."

Sunni thanked him and hurried around the front of the truck, glad that Jake had spent the day with his friend. It had done them both good. Running up the porch steps, she raced into the house for the camera. When she came back outside, Jake and Licorice were still playing. She watched them for a minute, amazed that the dog actually was playing tag with Jake. She took a picture of Licorice chasing Jake, and another of Jake laughing. When she zoomed in on Lic, the dog had a big grin on his face. There was no other way to describe it.

They spent the rest of the day being lazy, watching drag racing on television and later playing dominoes until bedtime.

On Sunday morning, they went to church with Lynda and Toby. The sheriff had to leave in the middle of the service because there was a break-in north of town. After they went home, they had what Jake called a scrounger's lunch, with each of them fixing themselves whatever they wanted to eat.

Mid-afternoon, Licorice woke Jake up from a nap in his recliner by making squeaking noises, indicating that he needed to go outside. Jake let him out, watching him from the screen porch. When the dog picked up a big rope pull toy and waggled it around in his mouth, Jake hollered, "Don't you know it's hot out there, dog?"

But he went outside anyway. Sunni followed with the camera. He grabbed one end of the toy and the tug-of-war was on, with Jake laughing and teasing the dog, and Licorice pulling for all he was worth, somehow growling at the same time. Jake leaned back slightly and dug in his heels. Licorice did the same, only with four feet. She focused the lens on Jake and, still looking through the camera, paused simply to enjoy his fun.

Suddenly, Licorice lost his grip and Jake stumbled, catching the heel of his boot on the garden hose. He fell backward, shock and pain flashing across his face as she snapped the picture.

A barrage of images bombarded Sunni's mind. Alan — blond, tan and handsome in a white tux, smiling tenderly as he watched her walk down the aisle on their wedding day. The two of them in a comfortable embrace on the beach, watching the dark blue waves of the Pacific. On assignment in Guatemala, Alan interviewing a local fruit vendor while Sunni snapped pictures of a beautiful bright green parrot with a yellow head.

Making chocolate-chip cookies with her mom, both of them giggling as they stole a bite of dough. Her father chasing their soap-covered golden retriever around a thick green lawn with the water hose, trying to rinse her off. Her younger sister, Courtney, running to her for a calming hug moments before her first date.

An old house surrounded by weeds, tall wild grass and a dusty road. Raised voices; men arguing. Then framed by her camera lens — one man shooting another, the victim flying backward. Men chasing her. The sound of gunfire. Running through a pasture, dodging cactus and mesquites, stumbling over rocks. A cliff . . . falling.

A dark Seattle street. Alan giving her a thumbs-up, holding his microphone and turning to a gang member. Sunni snapping a few pictures of them, then focusing solely on her husband. Gunshots! Alan falling backward. *Oh, dear God, so much blood. I can't make it stop. Please, God, make it stop. Agony, despair, unbearable heartache.*

"Alan . . ."

Sunni's keening cry made Jake's skin crawl. Lying on the ground to catch his breath, he raised up at her wail of agony. The camera slipped from her fingers, and she crumpled

281

to the patio.

Lynda came flying out the door. "Jake, what happened?" The screen door slammed shut as she knelt beside Sunni.

Jake scrambled to his feet and ran to the patio, ignoring the twinge in his knee. "She called out a man's name and fainted. I think her memory came back. Dr. Smith said it might be overwhelming." He knelt down and checked Sunni's pulse and breathing. Both were okay. "Let's get her inside where it's cooler."

Lynda jumped up and opened the screen door. "Should we call Doc Hampton?"

"If she doesn't regain consciousness in a few minutes." Jake lifted Sunni carefully, keeping her head lower than her knees. By the time he laid her on the couch and stuffed some pillows beneath her knees, she was beginning to come around. He desperately wanted to hold her but decided he'd better wait to see what she wanted. It wasn't his name she had screamed.

Sitting on the coffee table, he clasped her hand and gently brushed her hair back from her forehead. "Sugar, can you hear me?" She stirred, moving her head from side to side with a frown. "Come on, Sunni, open your eyes, talk to me."

Her eyelids fluttered and she looked up at

him, her face clouded with confusion. "I'm Carolyn . . . Carolyn Graham." Tears welled in her eyes.

"It'll be all right, sweetheart." When she tried to sit up, Jake gently pushed her back down on the couch. "Stay down for a few minutes. You fainted. Let your blood flow get back to normal and plenty of oxygen to your brain."

Lynda hovered behind the couch, gripping the top of the cushion and whispering a prayer. He brushed the moisture from Sunni's cheeks with his fingers, but her tears continued to flow. Pulling a tissue from the box on the table, he dabbed her face.

"Who is Alan?" He knew he probably should wait and let her tell him on her own, but he couldn't.

"My husband."

Jake's heart plummeted. *Oh, Father . . .*

Sunni squeezed her eyes shut, her breath catching on a little sob. "He was killed in a drive-by shooting two years ago."

"Sunni, I'm so sorry." His heart ached for her, for the pain she endured even now. She still loved her husband.

"It hurts so much." She sobbed, turning her face toward the back of the sofa.

"I know, sweetheart. I know." He pulled the pillows from beneath her knees and scooped her up in his arms. Turning around, he sat down on the sofa with her on his lap, cradling her to his heart. "Go ahead and cry, sugar. Let it out."

Lynda went into the kitchen. She returned a few minutes later and set a glass of water on the table and handed him a cool, damp cloth. "Do you want me to call Roberta?"

Jake nodded. The psychiatrist's card was on the refrigerator. "Call her cell number. We've never used it, so she may realize it's an emergency." When Lynda started to turn away, he held up his hand, asking her to wait. "Sunni, do you have your full memory back?"

"I think so." She took a deep, shuddering breath and wiped her cheek with trembling fingers.

"Can you remember what happened the day you were hurt?"

"Most of it." She frowned through her tears. "That night is still foggy."

"That's okay. If we call Toby, do you think you'll feel like talking to him this evening?"

"Maybe." Clutching his shirt, she buried her head on his shoulder with a sob. "I don't know."

"I'll call him and tell him what's happened," said Lynda. "He'll understand that she isn't ready to talk to him right now."

He half listened as Lynda made the calls in the kitchen. He was more concerned with trying to comfort Sunni than what the psychiatrist or sheriff would do. He carefully wiped her face with the cloth and coaxed her to take a small drink of the water.

A few minutes later, Lynda came back into the living room and perched on the seat of the rocker. "Roberta is coming down, but she has another client, so she probably won't get here until close to nine. I told her that Sunni was crying a lot but wasn't hysterical. Roberta said that was within the realm of normalcy, and that we didn't need to call Doc. Toby said he would come out when he's finished at the office. Not necessarily to try to get information about what happened to her unless she's up to it, but as a friend."

Lynda watched them for a minute, then stood. Jake noted the sheen of tears in her eyes. "I'm going to let y'all have some peace and quiet for a while. Holler if you need me for anything. I'll put fresh sheets on my bed for Roberta. I'll sleep on the Hide-A-Bed."

"You can have my room, and I'll sleep out here."

"Too many beds to change. I'll be fine here."

Jake didn't know how long he held Sunni, how long she cried. She drenched his shirt, but he didn't care if he had to wring it out and use a towel to dry off. Tears were supposed to be therapeutic, and he prayed it was true for Sunni. He murmured words of solace every now and then but questioned whether or not she even heard them. She clung to his shirt for a while before settling her hand on his shoulder.

He prayed that God would ease her pain as only He could, and that He would give her strength to deal with whatever lay before her. Given her reaction to her restored memories so far, he feared it would be a painful, difficult journey.

Jake held her until his arm ached and kept holding her when it went numb. He managed to stuff a couple of pillows beneath it for support. Gradually the feeling returned to it on jolts of pins and needles. Sunni eventually cried herself out, and her body relaxed as she fell asleep in his arms.

Lord, I don't want to ever let her go. But how could he possibly have a life with her when she was still so much in love with her husband? Alan. He'd considered it a nice name. Now it filled him with fear. How could he compete with a dead man?

■ ■ ■ ■

Sunni awoke to the mouthwatering aroma of frying teriyaki beef, making her stomach growl. Evidently her body functioned normally even when her brain was on overload. *Yuck, when did I start drooling in my sleep? And what did I do with my pillow?* The bed was wet beneath her face.

No, not the bed — Jake's shirt. His shoulder pillowed her head, and his arms encompassed her. He rested the side of his face on her hair, sheltering her in his gentle strength. She wanted to stay right there forever.

And lose him, too? The thought came swiftly and hit hard, tightening her stomach into a cold knot of fear.

When she stirred, Jake raised his head and loosened his hold. "How ya doin', sunshine?" he said softly. He'd used the same words and gentle tone when they finally let him in to see her at the emergency room the day he found her.

So much had changed since then. She had changed. She trusted the Lord again, and she'd found a new love. *Please God, don't let me return to the brokenhearted, tortured woman I was before. Please help me work through this fear.*

"Or should I call you Carolyn?"

She sat up and looked at him, saw the loving tenderness in his eyes and the fear. "I like Sunni better. Sunni was happy."

"And Carolyn wasn't?"

"No." She shoved her hair out of her face and winced at the sore muscles in her back. Stretching, she glanced at the mantel clock. It was almost five-thirty. "How long have we been sitting here?"

"I'm not sure. Maybe an hour and a half." He smiled, though he seemed sad. "Long enough that if I don't move, it'll take a week to get the kinks out."

"Me, too."

He lifted her off his lap and onto the couch. She sat there for a minute, still struggling to control all the memories and emotions whirling around in her mind and heart. But she didn't feel as overwhelmed as she had when they came crashing back. Jake stood, stretched and offered her his hand to help her up. She made her way around the coffee table, meeting Lynda and Toby as they came into the living room from the kitchen.

"How are you, hon?" Lynda gave her a gentle hug.

"Tired, rattled and hungry." Sunni forced

a smile, though she knew it probably looked as halfhearted as it felt.

"Go wash your face, and I'll finish up supper. We're dying to know all about you, but it won't kill us to wait until Dr. Smith gets here. That way you can tell your tale once and be done with it."

"Roberta is on her way?" She vaguely remembered Lynda mentioning the psychiatrist earlier, but she'd been too upset to understand what she said.

"Yes. I called her. She had a client appointment, so she's probably leaving her office right about now. She probably won't be here until eighty-thirty or nine."

Sunni went to the bathroom and washed her face. Staring in the mirror at her swollen eyes, red nose and blotchy, crinkled cheek, probably from a wrinkle in Jake's shirt, she wondered how long she had cried. She gripped the edge of the sink and closed her eyes. *Alan.* Oh, how she had loved him. They had been friends all through high school, fell in love in college, and had seven wonderful years of marriage. She would always love him.

The pain of his death seemed new and raw, her grief a deep, yawning hole in her heart. She had never worked through it. Blaming God for her beloved's murder, she had turned away from the Lord's strength and comforting love. She'd become almost like a robot, distancing herself from family and friends, immersing herself in building a new career and burying the pain until it came close to destroying her heart and soul.

How ironic that the night before she became lost on the Rocking K and fought so hard to survive, she had poured a bottle of sleeping pills into her hand and contemplated suicide. "No wonder You had to do something drastic, Lord." Tears stung her eyes again. "Thank You."

There was a soft knock on the bathroom door. "Sugar, are you okay?"

Sunni quickly dried her eyes and opened the door. "I look a fright, but I think I can hold myself together. I really need to brush my hair." He'd changed from his green Western shirt into a dark blue T-shirt. The salty wet cloth couldn't have been comfortable.

"Go ahead. Lynda said supper will be ready in a few minutes."

Sunni hurried to her bedroom and ran a brush through her hair, stopping a few times to work through tangles. Touching the pearl on her necklace, then tracing the outline of Texas, she whispered, "Guide me, Lord. Help me to do what is right. Help me resist the urge to run away again — not that I know how I'd manage it anyway."

Exhaling with a whoosh, she thought of several business items that needed to be taken care of the following day. One thing needed to be handled immediately, but she supposed the investigation could wait until after supper. Especially since the shooting had happened about a month earlier.

CHAPTER SEVENTEEN

When they were all seated and had joined hands, Jake asked the blessing on the food. "Lord, we also thank You that Sunni's memory has returned. We ask You to be with her and guide us to help her in anyway that we can. In Jesus' name, amen."

Spooning some rice onto her plate, Sunni glanced at Jake, then Toby. She handed the bowl to Jake. "The day I got lost, I witnessed a crime. A man was shot."

Jake paused, a spoonful of rice midair over his plate, his eyes narrowing as he stared at her. "You what?"

"Where?" Toby dished up some of the teriyaki beef and vegetables and handed the casserole to Lynda.

"I can't tell you exactly where it was, but I can give you a general idea of the location."

"How were you involved?" asked the sheriff.

"It was a wrong place, wrong time type of thing. I'm a professional photographer, specializing in scenic and documentary fine art."

"I knew it." Lynda nodded emphatically.

Sunni automatically put some honeydew chunks into the small bowl beside her plate and passed the fruit bowl on to Jake. "I was driving around, doing a little exploring, looking for some good pictures.

"I found the Granger Cemetery and stayed there for a while. After I went back to the highway, I turned south and drove a mile or two. I took a dirt road to the west and spotted an old house in some mesquite trees. There weren't any No Trespassing signs on the fence, so I drove across the cattle guard. There was an old wagon a little way from the road, so I stopped there and got out to walk around."

Toby looked at Jake. "Sounds like the old Parker place."

"That's what I'm thinking." Jake turned to Sunni. "It was an old homestead back around 1900. Caleb's grandfather bought the land from the heirs about twenty years ago."

"I took some pictures of the wagon and the front of the house." When Lynda handed the teriyaki stir-fry to her, Sunni added some to her plate and set the casserole on the table between her and Jake. It didn't seem strange to be talking about such a thing in the midst of a meal. When she and Alan had been together with friends, many of them also journalists, the stories swapped around the table often involved reporting on a crime or an adventure of some sort.

"I walked around toward the back of the house and heard men arguing. I used to be a photojournalist, and my reporter's instincts kicked in. I peeped around the corner of the house to see what was going on. It was a drug deal. So I started taking pictures. I got close-ups of each of the four men involved, then backed the zoom off a little to get the two men who were arguing."

"You stayed there and took pictures of a drug transaction?" Toby stared at her, his voice incredulous.

Sunni shrugged and gave him a mildly sheepish smile. "That was the kind of thing I did for five years. It was automatic. I didn't even think about it."

"Or of getting out of there, either." Jake appeared irritated.

"Well, I did think about that. I planned to take the picture of the drugs and money changing hands, then beat feet back to my

SUV as stealthily and quickly as possible. But the buyer didn't like the asking price. The dealer drew a gun and was waving it around, shouting threats and stomping his feet. The other guy got scared. He pulled a gun out from underneath his shirt, probably from his waistband and shot the dealer. In the chest, I think."

Jake almost dumped the teriyaki on the table. "You witnessed a murder?"

"He might have been hit in the shoulder. I couldn't tell exactly from where I was. I don't know if he killed him or just wounded him." She rested her hand on the table, absently smoothing the fringe on the place mat. "I was taking a picture as he pulled the trigger, and it startled me so much that I made a noise."

"You yelled?"

"More of a scared-out-of-my-wits yelp. But they heard me. I started running back toward my SUV but one of them came around the house and blocked my way. So I took off through the pasture with two of them chasing me." Reliving those moments made her shiver. She closed her eyes for a second, and Jake instantly covered her hand with his. Gathering her composure, she looked at him. "I threw my camera into the middle of a giant prickly pear cactus and kept running. I figured I could retrieve it later."

"If you got away from them," Jake said with a scowl.

"Right. I wasn't really thinking details one way or the other. One guy was shooting, up in the air, I think. I ran a zigzag pattern just in case he decided to point the gun at me. Learned that trick when we were running from the coyotes in Mexico."

Jake groaned and released her hand. "I assume you mean the two-legged kind."

"That's right. The guys who smuggle illegal immigrants across the border. Alan —" she shifted her gaze to Toby "— my husband, was a journalist. We were in Mexico working on a story about their smuggling operation. They didn't like it much."

"I reckon not." Toby shook his head and took a bite of beef.

"Anyway, back to the old house. I was running as fast as I could. I glanced back to see how close they were, and the next thing I knew I was flying off a cliff. I tried to tuck and roll. The dirt was soft when I first landed, but I obviously hit my head on something hard. There are some fuzzy memories about the night, mostly stumbling around in the dark, being scared, my head about to explode and being sick to my stomach. But that's basically all I remember until the next morning. When I woke up, I was at the bottom of a high, steep canyon and had a horrible headache."

"So you started walking, trying to find a way out." Toby glanced at the clock. "If we cut through the Rocking K, we should be able to do a preliminary check on the Parker place before nightfall. Sunni, are you up to going with us to confirm we're in the right place?"

"Yes. But you guys check behind that house before I go around there. I don't want to look at a dead body if there is one."

"All you need to do is tell us if we're where we should be," said Jake, calling Caleb to let him know what was going on.

They fell silent, concentrating on finishing the meal quickly. When they were done, Lynda left the remaining food in the serving dishes and stuck them in refrigerator. Jake called Roberta to let her know they were leaving and to tell her that the back door wouldn't be locked in case they weren't home when she got there.

They picked Caleb up on the way. Sunni suspected that Jake drove faster than he normally would on the rough dirt road crossing the Rocking K. They bounced around a lot more than usual. She sat in the back seat with Licorice, so Caleb could have the extra leg room in the front. Lynda rode with Toby in his patrol car.

They crossed the ranch to the highway, drove north about a mile and turned up a dirt road. Sunni recognized the entrance to the old homestead when they reached the cattle guard. "This is it. I took a picture of a pretty red bird near the big clump of mistletoe in that mesquite." Her pulse kicked into high gear and her palms grew sweaty. *Please, Lord, don't let us find a body here.*

Jake drove up to the front of the house and stopped. Toby pulled in beside him. Jake turned to Sunni. "Are you all right?"

"So far. But I'm not budging out of this truck until you tell me to."

"I'll be back as quick as I can." He hopped out of the truck, letting Toby lead the way.

Jake returned a few minutes later, walking around to her open window. "No body. Can you show me where the camera is?"

"Yes."

He opened the back truck door, helping her down. Leaning in, he pulled a pair of leather work gloves from a pocket in the back of the driver's seat before he shut the door again.

Sunni pointed toward an old barn mostly hidden by mesquites. "It's over there."

"Do you think your camera would survive a downpour?" They walked through the grass and weeds toward the barn. "We had a gully-washer the night I found you."

"I don't know. The specs didn't say anything about it being waterproof. But the cactus is partly under the eve. It might have been somewhat protected from the rain."

It took a few minutes to find the camera when they reached the barn. It had fallen next to the building, lying on a big prickly pear pad, held in place by the spines. Not only the barn but also the cactus pads higher up had protected it from the rain.

Jake carefully retrieved the camera and handed it to Sunni. "It doesn't look any worse for wear." A smile lit his eyes, and she had a glimpse of the lawman — one pleased with an element of an investigation. "You didn't mention that it was digital."

"I didn't think of it."

They walked back to the house, where Toby was checking the ground. Caleb and Lynda stood off to one side watching him.

"Did you find anything?" Sunni gripped the camera, nervously scanning the area. She hadn't said anything to Jake, but she wondered if wild animals might have made off with the body. It was a gruesome thought.

Toby looked at the sun, low on the horizon. "We'll have to do a more thorough investigation in the morning, but so far I haven't seen any indication that someone was killed here. Don't misunderstand, I believe you saw someone shot. But I don't think they left him behind, which means he was likely injured, not dead. I see you found the camera." The same light of potential success gleamed in Toby's eyes. "Digital?"

"Yes. I haven't tried it yet in case the batteries are low." Sunni pushed the button and it came on. "It's working." She retrieved the last picture, swallowed hard and held the camera so Toby could see the LED screen. Jake looked over her shoulder, then rested his hand on her back when he saw that the picture was of the shooting.

"The guy with the gun is Ben Alder," said Toby. "I arrested him and a cohort three years ago for trying to rob the truck stop. Easiest arrest I ever made. A couple of truckers had them hogtied by the time we arrived. He spent some time in prison but obviously not long enough." Sunni moved to the earlier close-up pictures, and Toby grumbled under his breath. "That's his friend, Reggie Compton. I don't know the drug dealer or his accomplice.

"If I can borrow this, I'll send these

pictures to law enforcement in neighboring counties. I expect somebody will know who the dealer and his friend are. Compton and Alder are probably still in the area. They don't seem to wander too far from family and friends."

She handed him the camera. "I'll do whatever I can to help you arrest and convict them."

Roberta was waiting for them when they returned to the ranch house. She hugged Sunni and listened quietly as Jake related what Sunni had told them and what they had found at the old house.

The psychiatrist smiled at Toby as they all settled in the living room. "It's not every day you have a picture of the crime."

"No, ma'am, it's not. Usually, we're only that fortunate if somebody robs a store and they have security cameras." He turned to Sunni. "I know everybody, myself included, wants to know some of your history, but so I won't forget about them, there are some practical matters we should go over. If that's agreeable with you, Roberta."

"I don't have any problem it. When the business things are out of the way, Sunni can tell us whatever she wants to about herself." She smiled at Sunni. "Not only do

I want to know you better, but I have a theory about what caused your amnesia. I'm curious to see if the facts support my idea."

Toby took a small notepad from his shirt pocket. "What kind of vehicle were you driving?"

"A 2006 GMC red Yukon. Washington plates." She rattled off the license number and paused as Toby wrote down the information. "I travel all over for my photography and seldom stay in one place very long. Both my car and my driver's license are still registered in Washington."

Sitting beside her on the sofa, Jake ran his finger over the tip of her thumb. "It sure would make it easier if all the states included thumbprints in the driver's license database the way Texas does."

"Using the license plate number, we might be able to locate your Yukon, or what's left of it, if it's been stripped." Toby glanced at her as she winced. "I know. Not a pleasant thought, but to be honest, a likely one. That's a nice SUV, though. There might be a market for it among stolen car connoisseurs. But they'll change the plates if they sell it."

"I'll need to file an insurance claim either way."

"Right. Were you staying in the area?"

"At a house in Abilene. It belongs to a friend of a friend who is in England with his work until October. The key was on my keychain, but there wasn't anything in my purse or other gear with the address."

"No mail?" asked Toby.

"All my mail goes to a box with a service in Seattle. They weed out the junk mail and hold anything else until I call to tell them to send it to me General Delivery wherever I am at the time. I pay my bills either online or by automatic deduction from my bank account."

"Is all that on your computer?" asked Jake.

"I keep my account in Quicken, but I don't have any account numbers listed anywhere on the computer. I do the banking online with a special identification number and password. I type them in each time. It's not set to remember them automatically."

"What about a checkbook?" Jake had taken over the questioning. Sunni doubted he even realized he was usurping Toby's job. The sheriff didn't seem to mind. In fact, he looked mildly amused as he took notes.

"No checkbook. I use a debit card or one credit card. I have all the information on those in a file at the house. My insurance stuff, too." Thinking of the financial mess she might be in made her grimace. Some places weren't set up for debit cards and treated them as credit cards, requiring a signature instead of a PIN number. Other places automatically ran it as a credit unless they were told differently. "When I get the card numbers tomorrow, I'll call the bank and see if I have any money left in my bank account. And if I owe a fortune on the credit card."

"How will you get into the house?" asked Lynda.

"A neighbor has a key. They knew I might not be there much, so they're looking after the place."

"You may be able to dispute any credit card debt that's run up. Hopefully, you can work with the bank regarding your checking account. Unfortunately, banks aren't always as sympathetic as we'd like when it comes to identity theft." Jake frowned, still toying with her fingers. "Was your pin number for the debit card in your purse or anywhere in your SUV?"

"No." Sunni tapped her forehead with the fingers of her free hand. "It's up here. Nowhere else. So they would have to use the debit card like a credit card. At least they couldn't use it in an ATM."

"Unfortunately, a lot of stores don't check

for identification when people use credit cards. Most will check to see if the signature matches, though. We'll get hoppin' on this stuff in the morning."

"You told Jake that your name was Carolyn Graham," said Toby. "Your SUV and driver's license are registered in Washington. Is that D.C. or Washington state?"

"State. I was born and raised in Seattle. My parents and younger sister still live there."

"That should take care of the business end of it for now." Toby nodded to Roberta. "She's all yours."

The doctor nodded her thanks and smiled kindly at Sunni. "Do you feel like sharing more about yourself? Or are you too tired?"

"I'm tired, but too keyed up to sleep anyway. I can talk for a little while." She felt Jake's fingers go still on hers. "I graduated from the University of Washington with a double major in journalism and photography." She smiled at him. "I went there partly on a softball scholarship."

He chuckled and tickled her palm with his fingertip. "No wonder you played like a pro at Caleb's."

"You took all the natural talent the Lord gave you and fine-tuned it." Lynda beamed at her like a proud mama. "Good for you."

"I was a photojournalist, and as I said earlier, Alan was a journalist. We worked as a team at *The Seattle Times* for a while, and a stint with *Newsweek* for about a year. Then we did freelance articles for a variety of magazines. Two years ago we were working on an article about gang violence in Seattle. He was interviewing one of the gang leaders, and I was taking photos when he was killed in a drive-by shooting."

"He's the man in your dream?" asked Roberta.

Sunni nodded. "Yes. After he was killed, I left Seattle and changed careers to fine-art photography. In the last year and a half I've worked in four states and two foreign countries."

"You were taking his picture at the time of the shooting?"

"Yes." Sunni drew a deep breath to steady herself. She didn't like to go into detail about that night. She'd gone through far too much of it during the trial of the man who killed Alan. And in her dreams.

"You were also snapping a picture of the man at the old Parker place when he was shot, right?" Roberta watched her carefully.

"Yes."

"And you were taking pictures today when your memory returned?"

Sunni realized where the doctor was leading. "Yes. I was focused on Jake when Licorice lost his grip on the toy. Jake fell backward, a shocked expression on his face. Pain, too." She glanced at him. "Did you hurt your leg?"

"For a minute." He turned his attention to Roberta. "So Sunni's amnesia is connected with the pictures?"

"Yes, I believe it is. The first and worst trauma happened when you were taking Alan's picture and captured the image of him being killed. It's an image that will be in your mind's eye forever. When you snapped the picture of the other man being shot, then were chased, fell and were injured, it brought back the trauma, fear and horror of Alan's death. It all added up to more than you could handle emotionally, so your mind blocked out your memories to protect you."

"Jake falling while I was taking his picture was somehow the trigger to bring back my memory."

"That's right. Remember I told you that sometimes returning to the place where you lost your memory would bring it back? Basically that's what you did with the camera. Only in your case, the *place* was the action as seen through the camera's viewfinder or

LED. Both make rectangular frames around the scene. The scenes were similar — they all happened suddenly, the men were hurt in some way and they fell backward."

"That's wild," muttered Lynda.

"Unusual, yes. But it fits the pattern. If your mind and emotions hadn't sufficiently healed, then seeing Jake fall today wouldn't have brought your memory back. Because you care about him, it might have even prolonged your memory loss, perhaps permanently."

"If something like that happens again, I'm not going to go blank again, am I?"

"I doubt it. If the trauma is great enough, it's possible. But God has been at work here, too, not just your mind. We'll leave you in His hands."

"A very good place to be." Sunni was thankful that God had provided her with a Christian counselor. She expected a lot of psychiatrists wouldn't acknowledge Him or His care.

"Yes, it is." The psychiatrist yawned. "I'm worn-out, and I know you must be exhausted. I'm for going to bed."

Toby looked at his watch. "Gettin' real close to my bedtime. I'd better head on down the road." When he stood, Lynda did, too. "I'll run a check on your plates tomorrow and get those pictures out to other agencies in the area. I'll holler if I learn anything."

"Thank you, Toby. You're terrific."

"Isn't he, though?" Lynda hooked her arm through his. "I'll walk you out to the car."

"Yes, ma'am." A sparkle lit his eyes as he picked up his hat and they walked out the front door.

"I'd like to go out on the back porch for a few minutes and look at the stars," said Sunni. "Unwind a little bit."

"I'll go with you." Jake stood and pulled her up beside him.

They strolled out back, standing at the edge of the screen porch, looking up at the stars. Light from the house faintly illuminated the porch. Jake put his arm around Sunni's shoulders, holding her close against his side.

"In some ways, I almost wish my memories hadn't returned. I was happy here with you."

"That doesn't have to change." His voice was deep, husky with emotion.

"I have to go to Abilene. All the insurance and bank information is there."

"We'll go over there tomorrow, but I think you should come back here, for a while anyway. Until you get things sorted out."

"Things?" She looked up at him, her heart melting at the tenderness in his eyes and his wistful expression.

"You, me, the gallery. The past, the future." He paused. "Life."

She smiled and leaned her head against his shoulder. "Just life, huh?"

His arm tightened. "And what makes it worth living."

CHAPTER EIGHTEEN

Exhaustion didn't mean sleep came easily. Sunni felt as if a floodgate had been opened, allowing a deluge of memories to pour in. Along with them came insight into her mistakes in trying to deal with Alan's death. It was as if God had to wipe the mirror clean so that she could see the reflection of her life more clearly.

Although she had walked away from God, His love had remained true and strong. Instead of punishing her for disobedience and bitterness, He had moved her from a wilderness of the soul to an actual dry, dusty land, where the only certain things were His love and protection. He had provided people to care for her, even love her. He had given her freedom from pain so that she might begin to heal and restore the depth of her faith. He was renewing her heart and trust, both in Him and her fellowman. He showed her that she could love again.

But did she want to? Did she want to commit to a lasting relationship with Jake? Could she bear the pain it might bring? A fresh wave of grief for Alan swept through her, breaking her heart all over again. Sobbing, she buried her face in the pillow, afraid Licorice would hear her and bring Jake to check on her.

When her tears were spent, she whispered, "I take comfort, Jesus, knowing that Alan is with You. I should rejoice for his sake that he's strolling in heaven at Your side. He loved You so much. He must be so happy, but that doesn't mean I don't miss him.

"I know You've given me Jake, that You've chosen him for me. Not to replace Alan, because no one ever could, but to fill the emptiness and loneliness in my life. I don't want to be scared, yet the fear is still there, lurking in the shadows. Give me courage, Lord. Help me to trust You as much in this part of my life as I do in others."

The fear of losing someone else she deeply cared about had driven her from the loving arms of her family. She'd thought if she moved far enough away and only talked to them a couple of times a year, it wouldn't hurt as much if they died. Now, she realized that the pain would be even greater because of all the companionship and love she had denied them and herself. She glanced at the clock. Eleven-thirty Texas time was nine-thirty in Seattle. Her folks seldom went to bed before ten. Often later.

Sunni hopped out of bed, grabbing her cotton bathrobe and slipping it on. Opening her door quietly, she tiptoed down the hall. Lynda slept soundly on the sofa, so Sunni went to the kitchen for the cordless phone Jake kept there on a charger. When she crept back down the hallway, Jake was leaning against the door frame to her room. Barefoot and his hair all rumpled, he wore a white T-shirt and dark green running shorts. The man looked good even when he was half-asleep.

Light from the night-light in her room spilled into the hallway. He glanced at the phone and smiled lazily. "Callin' your broker?" he asked, barely above a whisper.

"My folks. I'm ashamed to admit I haven't talked to them in six months. They don't even know I'm in Texas. I'll pay you for the long-distance charges."

He ducked his head slightly. "You think I care about that?"

"No." After all he had done for her, she felt chagrined. "Of course not. That's something Carolyn would say. Not Sunni."

"So I have to deal with split personalities now?"

"Maybe for a little while until I get them rolled into one." She made a face. "That's kind of weird, isn't it?"

"Yeah. But I love you anyway." He drew a quick breath, as if he hadn't intended to say that.

His tone had been teasing. His reaction wasn't. She believed his feelings went much deeper. Shouldn't she be honest with him?

"I love you, too, Jake," she finally whispered.

He pushed away from the door frame, taking a step closer. "I hear some reservation."

"I haven't had much time to sort things out."

"True." He cupped her face with one hand. "Maybe this will help."

Leaning down, he gave her plenty of opportunity to pull away, but at that moment, running was the last thing she wanted to do. Touching her only with his hand and his lips, he kissed her tenderly, with slow thoroughness and profound love.

Oh, my.

He raised his head, trailing his fingertips down the side of her face. "Go mend your fences, sweetheart. Talk all night if you want to. I'll tell Lic that you're on the phone, so when he hears your voice, he doesn't need to worry."

"Give him a pat on the head for me." She was surprised she could utter a coherent sentence.

"Will do. See you in the morning," he added with a yawn as she stepped into her bedroom. "Not too early."

"Definitely." Sunni closed her door and made her way across the room on wobbly legs. It wasn't merely his kiss that made her weak and her heart pound. Though the physical contact was certainly part of it, the intensity of his love touched the depths of her being.

She and Alan had loved greatly, but their relationship had been completely different, more of a comfortable companionship. Perhaps it was because they had been close friends for so many years before they married. They had thrived on the adventurous, fast pace of their jobs. Even then, she had sometimes wondered if their marriage would last if they ever tried an ordinary, less dangerous form of work.

Jake was her friend and confidant, too, yet there was a power in their love that she had never imagined could exist. By his very nature, he was a protector, steady and reliable. Life with him might not be adventurous, but it would never be boring. Not when the pleasure of his smile, the timbre of his voice or his loving touch filled her heart with joy.

Crawling up on the bed, she reminded herself this wasn't a decision to be made quickly. She dialed her parents' phone number and felt her throat clog up.

"Hello." Her mom's voice wrapped her in a cocoon of warmth and comfort.

"Hi, Mom."

"Carolyn, what's wrong?" Trust her mother to pick up on her feelings immediately.

"Nothing now, but the last several weeks have been interesting." Sunni cleared her throat, wishing she could give her mother a hug right then. Dad, too. "It's a long story, so tell me how y'all are doing first."

"Y'all? Where are you? I didn't recognize the phone number on caller ID."

"Texas."

"Well, you're picking up the accent." Her mom laughed. "We're fine. Plugging along in the same routine. Dad has been real busy at Boeing. I'm still working two days a week at the vet's. Courtney and Paul are buying a house out near Lake Tapps. Your dad is in here now, so I'll put you on the speaker phone. Tell us what's going on, dear."

"First, I want to apologize for staying away and for not keeping in touch, for shutting you out of my life. It was nothing you've done. I love you as much as ever. I just couldn't stay in Seattle. I thought that by running away and breaking the ties with my past, I could bury my pain. And I thought if I wasn't so close to you, then if something happened to you, it wouldn't hurt as much." She swallowed hard, hoping she could get through the conversation without bawling like a little kid.

"Honey, we figured it might be something like that, but we've been so worried about you." Her father's voice was thick with emotion. "Especially when you haven't returned most of our calls."

"I know you have, and I'm sorry for putting you through it. Can you forgive me?"

"Of course," said her dad.

"You know we do. We were so frustrated not knowing how to help you." Her mom sniffed.

"God was the only One who could, I think. I'm in West Texas. I came down here to shoot some photographs, but He had something else in mind." Stuffing another pillow behind her back, she leaned against the headboard and told them almost everything that had happened. She didn't mention the more personal interaction between her and Jake, but she expected her mom, and maybe even her dad, could read between the lines.

After they had reacted as expected to all she'd been through, her mom said, "Jake sounds like a fine man. Are you in love with him, Carolyn?"

"Yes, ma'am."

"Ma'am? Is that a Texas thing, too?"

"Yeah." Sunni grinned and shifted her position. They'd been talking for an hour.

"Is he in love with you?"

"Yes —"

Her father interrupted. "And you two are living in the same house?"

Sunni pictured his concerned expression. Always the protector. Jake reminded her of him. Her dad was also a man who expected high morals from his daughters. "Yes, sir. But his aunt is here, too. She wouldn't put up with any hanky-panky." At least nothing beyond kissing and hugging. "Not that Jake has tried anything. He's a lot like you, a God-loving, honorable man."

"Are you two going to get married?" asked her mom.

"He hasn't proposed, but I think he'd like to. He's trying to give me time to sort some things out."

"He loves you. You love him. He's a Christian, and by your account a fine man —"

Sunni interrupted, "By all accounts."

"By all accounts, a fine man who owns a successful ranch. So you probably won't starve and will always have a roof over your head. Besides, you're successful, too. You probably earn as much or more than he does." Her mother paused for a second. "Does he like kids?"

"He adores his friend's boys."

"Does he want a family of his own?"

"We haven't talked about it, but I expect so." She uncomfortably understood the reasons behind her mother's questions. Sunni had wanted children. Alan had been adamantly against it. He hadn't wanted anything to interfere with their careers. They were a couple and a team, and that was the way he wanted it to remain.

"Child of mine, what is there to sort out?"

"I don't think I could bear it if something happened to him."

"None of us knows what tomorrow will bring," her father said quietly. "You take the blessings God gives you and treasure them. Trust the Lord with all your heart and don't lean on your own understanding, honey. It seems to me that God brought you and Jake together. Don't throw away His gift."

"Daddy, how come you're so wise?"

Her father made a little sound, then cleared his throat. "You haven't called me Daddy since you were a little girl."

"I did a lot of times in my heart. Uh-oh, I'm getting all sappy. It's almost one o'clock here. I'd better go to sleep. I have to deal with the bank and insurance tomorrow . . . today. I want to come see you, soon. Maybe in a week or so, if I have any money left."

"If you don't, you let us know. We'll pay your airfare home and help you out any way we can." Her dad always had been generous, though practical.

"Bring Jake with you." Excitement bubbled in her mom's voice. "We want to meet him and thank him for rescuing you — in more ways than one."

"I'll give you a call when I know how things are going. I love you. Give my love to Courtney, too. Tell her I'll call her in a day or two."

After her folks said their goodbyes, Sunni hung up the phone and set it on the nightstand. She turned out the lamp and snuggled down in the bed. "Maybe Mom's right. What is there to sort out?"

For the first time in two years, she fell asleep with peace in her heart and mind.

■ ■ ■ ■

The next morning, Jake drove her to Abilene. Armed with all her account numbers and paperwork, she reported her Yukon and its contents stolen, and talked to the cell-phone company, bank and credit-card company. To her great relief, a couple of astute salesclerks had alerted the bank and credit-card company when they suspected identity theft.

The first time the crooks tried to use her debit card, apparently having a female accomplice make the purchase, she told the clerk that it was a credit card. The man questioned her signature because it wasn't even close to the one on the card. When he asked to see identification, the woman left the burritos, potato chips and Twinkies on the convenience store counter and ran from the store. When notified, the bank blocked the use of the debit card and sent Sunni a letter advising her of the situation.

The thieves had managed a few transactions with the credit card, running up four hundred dollars in charges, before the cashier at a restaurant in San Angelo became suspicious. The criminals were more brazen that time, with their female friend actually using Sunni's driver's license as identification.

But the cashier didn't go for it. Though the accomplice had blond hair, her eyes were brown and she was a good four inches taller in low-heeled sandals than Sunni's five-feet-four-inch height. As the restaurant worker told the police and credit-card company, the woman didn't look anything like the picture on the driver's license, which she thought was a good one, by the way.

The woman claimed to have picked up her sister's purse by mistake, and her boyfriend, who according to his description probably was Ben Alder, paid the bill in cash. They fled before the police arrived, but the cashier kept Sunni's credit card. The company had frozen the account immediately.

Sunni was surprised to learn that the thieves hadn't run up a huge cell-phone bill. In fact, it appeared that they had barely used it at all. Jake decided that they were afraid the authorities might be able to find them by tracing the cell phone calls.

They went by the post office and picked up her mail, which included the notification from the bank of suspicious activity on her debit card. After lunch, they visited pawnshops around town in the hope of finding some of her things, particularly her photo equipment. But they came up empty-handed.

After loading the rest of her belongings in Jake's truck, Sunni gave the house key to the neighbor. She had no intention of returning there, though she didn't know how long she'd remain at Jake's. *Forever* was her heart's desire, but since he hadn't actually proposed, she didn't quite know how to broach the subject. She supposed she could just blurt it out. *Hey, cowboy, I love you and I want to marry you.* But she never wanted him to feel as if he had been pushed into marriage.

As they drove back to the ranch, Jake focused on the road and didn't seem interested in conversation. After being on the phone so long that morning, she was all talked out. The late night and quiet hum of the pickup soon lulled her to sleep.

One part of Jake's mind concentrated on driving, but the rest of it swirled with turmoil. Was his house a temporary resting place before she took off for parts unknown? Was he temporary? Or was the love they shared strong enough to make her settle down? Did she have room in her heart to share her life with another man? Or would Alan's memory always hang over them, keeping them from true happiness?

Lord, it seems to me that You went to a lot of trouble to bring us together. I told her I wasn't going to push her, and I'm not. But I'm not letting her leave without her knowing exactly how I feel. He was going to ask her to marry him. If she refused, it would break his heart, but that was a risk he had to take. *Let me know when the time is right, Lord. I'm trusting in You, trusting that this is Your will for us.*

She woke up about twenty minutes later. Straightening, she yawned and stretched as much as possible within the confines of the seat belt and shoulder harness.

Jake glanced at her and smiled. "Good nap?"

"I stayed up too late talking to my parents."

"How did that go?" They'd been so busy all morning trying to think of everything she needed to do and then doing it that he hadn't had a chance to ask.

"Great. My parents are very loving and kind. Forgiving comes easy for them. My sister is married so I didn't get to talk to her. It was too late to call her by the time my folks and I hung up. I think we'll be all right, too. I'll give her a call tonight. I told them I'd probably go home next week. I really want to spend some time with them."

She's leaving. Jake's pulse kicked into overdrive. Would she come back? Not if he didn't ask her to. He spotted a little rest stop ahead, nothing more than a covered picnic table and a big mesquite tree for shade. Slowing, he pulled off the road into the parking space, rolled down the windows and turned off the engine.

When he unfastened his seat belt and turned toward Sunni, she studied his face, then unfastened her seat belt, too. "What's on your mind?"

"You, me, us."

"And what makes life worth living?" Her smile drew him closer.

"That's right." He noted the rapid pulse beating in her throat. "You know I love you." She nodded and shifted toward him slightly. "And you love me." She nodded again, her eyes sparkling. He relaxed a little bit. "I need a good cook." Her eyebrow went up. "And somebody to drive the pickup and pull the trailer when I'm moving cattle." She glanced behind the truck but didn't say anything. "And help me take care of Licorice and feed carrots to the horses."

He leaned toward her, his gaze dropping

to her mouth. "Someone to share sunrises, sunsets, falling stars and beautiful pictures." He whispered a kiss against her lips. "And kids." When he pulled back to look into her eyes, they glistened with moisture. "I want to sit on the porch with you when we're old, and to love you and live with you all the years between now and then. Will you marry me, Sunni?"

"Yes. Oh, yes!"

When she put her arms around his neck and kissed him, he knew he would never have to worry about the shadows of her past. They sat there in the shade, a little breeze blowing through the open windows, and made plans for the future between kisses. They were back to the kissing part when Jake heard a car door slam.

Releasing Sunni, he straightened, a little embarrassed to be caught smooching by the side of a public highway. He checked the rearview mirror and saw Toby adjust his hat before he started toward them. "Uh-oh, we're in trouble now. Toby will never let us live this down."

Sunni grinned and smoothed her hair. "It would be worse if it was somebody else."

Toby walked up to the driver's-side door. He looked through the open window and nodded to Sunni, then turned his attention to Jake. He attempted a stern frown, but the twinkle in his eyes ruined it. "Good thing I'm not a bandito. I've been sitting back there for five minutes."

"Oops." Sunni giggled and hid her face against Jake's shoulder.

"We were celebrating our engagement." Jake grinned from ear to ear.

A broad smile spread across his friend's face. "Congratulations! I was beginning to think you were going to waltz across Texas before you got around to asking her." The sheriff scanned the area and laughed. "Son, on the romantic scale of places to propose, this ranks about a minus three."

"The time was right." Jake clasped Sunni's hand when she straightened and settled back in her seat. "What brings you out this way?"

"We caught Alder and Compton this morning. They were visiting Alder's sister north of town. I tried to call you a couple of times, but I couldn't raise you. After that I was in a dead spot."

"I forgot to charge my phone, then I hit a couple of no-service spots, too."

Toby looked at Sunni. "When I showed them the pictures of the shooting, they started talking faster than a machine gun, pleading self-defense. They didn't notice

Sunni's camera. They just knew that she'd seen Alder shoot the guy. The whole episode had them running scared and crazy. They swore up and down that they weren't trying to hurt her. They only meant to chase her away from the scene then run back and hightail it out of there ahead of her.

"They didn't think she was hurt when she fell. Figured she only had the wind knocked out of her because the ground looked soft. It never occurred to them that she couldn't climb out of the canyon or might die out there.

"Of course, the Yukon was too much of a temptation to leave. They figured she could catch a ride when she got back to the road. Those boys put together are about as sharp as a butter knife, so I'm inclined to believe them. They were smart enough to call their attorney, though, and work a deal."

"What kind of a deal?" Jake scowled at him. "They could have killed Sunni."

"The district attorney agreed not to charge them with attempted murder, both for Sunni and the drug dealer — who is alive and well, by the way — in exchange for leading them to the man who bought her SUV."

"What kind of cockeyed deal is that?" At Jake's raised voice, Sunni laid her hand on his arm.

"It was self-defense, and they never shot at me."

"They chased you off that cliff and left you. They could have killed you."

"I know." She sighed and moved her hand. "Toby, was the deal worth it?"

"That's debatable, but in the larger scheme of things, it probably is. I'll have to show you what I mean. Turn your rig around and follow me."

Grumbling the whole way, Jake followed Toby back down the highway. He turned off the road at the entrance to the Pendleton Ranch. Jake had met the owner, Todd Pendleton, but that was all. They followed Toby around the ranch house to a large barn. Law-enforcement vehicles from several departments, including the Texas Rangers, were parked around it.

Toby said something to one of the officers, then motioned for Jake and Sunni to go with him. When they walked into the barn, Jake slowly scrutinized the interior. "It looks like a regular barn, though bigger than most around here. Some stalls, miscellaneous farm equipment and a hayloft."

"It's anything but regular." Toby flipped a big lever on the wall, triggering the whirring sound of a motor. A minute later, a twenty-by-forty-foot wooden ramp slowly dropped from the first-floor ceiling.

"It's like a James Bond movie," murmured Sunni.

"Wait until you see what's upstairs."

Accompanied by a handful of officers, they walked up the ramp with Toby. At the top, they stopped and stared. The whole loft was filled with neatly parked vehicles and equipment-five pickups, a couple of cars, forklifts, bobcats, golf carts and lawn mowers. And one red 2006 Yukon.

"That's my Yukon! He hasn't even changed the license plates." She ran over to the SUV and opened the door, searching the inside. "I guess it was too much to hope that the rest of my camera equipment would still be here."

"Sorry, Sunni," said Toby. "Alder and Compton pawned it in San Angelo. I checked with the pawnshop, but it was sold a few days after they brought it in. There are four other buildings like this scattered around the ranch, all full of stolen property, including some of the vehicles stolen in the area."

"Organized crime?" asked Jake. When Toby nodded, Jake put his arm around Sunni. "At least you'll get your wheels back."

She smiled and slid her arm around his waist. "All in all, it's been a good day. Thanks, Lord."

"Amen and amen." Jake tipped her face up toward his and kissed her.

He heard a chuckle and opened one eye to see Toby herding the other officers back down the ramp.

EPILOGUE

On a mild early-October Saturday afternoon, Jake waited at the front of Kincaid
Community Church for his bride. Caleb
served as best man, and Toby was grooms-
man. Drew had been invited to be a junior
groomsmen and fidgeted a little beside
Toby. When Sunni had proclaimed that her
heart was set on the men wearing their dark
Western-style suits instead of tuxes, the
three grown-ups had cheered. Drew figured
his favorite red shirt, a new pair of jeans
and polished boots were sufficient, but his
mama bought him a nice new suit anyway.

Jake glanced around the packed church,
thankful for friends and Sunni's family. His
parents were close in his heart on this
special day, and he hoped that somehow
they knew of his happiness.

He caught a glimpse of Sunni's sister,
Courtney, standing on the porch and giggling, probably with Sunni. Those two

laughed a lot when they were together. They favored each other, except Courtney's hair was a light brown, as were her eyes.

Sunni's attendants had chosen dresses in various fall colors, coordinated with a jacket in a filmy, leafy-patterned material that picked up all the colors and then some. Sunni wanted something they could use later to wear to church or out for a nice evening.

The organist began to play, and Megan made her entrance, welcomed by a big grin and tiny wave from her son. Lynda came down the aisle next, and Jake glanced at Toby. Given the pride on the man's face, he expected an engagement announcement soon. Courtney, the matron of honor, wore a smile a mile wide as she passed Jake.

The ring bearers, Cody and Licorice, took their places in the doorway. Jake saw Sunni's hand reach out and adjust the little white satin scarf around Licorice's neck, then pat him on the head. As the dubious duo started down the aisle, she peeked around the door frame to watch them with a watery smile. Both the boy and the dog seemed to take their assignments seriously, even though the rings attached to the scarf Lic wore and the pillow Cody carried were fake. The real wedding rings were safely in

Caleb's and Courtney's care.

Then Sunni and her father stepped through the doorway, and Jake only had eyes for his love. She wore an off-white, short-sleeved silk dress with a soft flowing skirt that stopped at mid-calf. She'd wanted something she could wear again, too. Skipping the veil, she had draped the sides of her gleaming blond hair back with sapphire-and-amethyst clips that had belonged to her grandmother. The Concho pearl Texas pendant adorned her neck. She also wore lavender Concho pearl earrings, his wedding gift to her.

She stopped at his side, her eyes and face glowing with love. After she handed her multicolored rose bouquet to Courtney, her father gave her away, putting her hand in Jake's and briefly placing his own over theirs in blessing.

Turning to face Jake, Sunni met his gaze, her heart soaring at the love she saw there. She touched the pearl at her throat then laid her hand over his heart.

She was home at last.

Dear Reader,

I was writing a Scottish historical when a modern-day Texan galloped into my imagination. Whoa, cowboy! Wrong country, wrong century. I told Jake to go herd some cows, but he camped out in a corner of my mind instead. Occasionally, he'd saunter by, reminding me that there was a young lady lost on his ranch. He really needed to rescue her, and God had a story of love, healing and forgiveness for me to tell.

I kept writing historicals, including two for Steeple Hill Books, *Twice Blessed* and *Standing Tall.* Finally the time was right to return to the modern era. My dear cowboy was so relieved.

We are greatly blessed to have a God who loves us, who is our help in times of trouble and who forgives our sins and mistakes if we come to Him with a contrite heart. I pray that you have a loving relationship with Him.

I hope the Lord will touch you in some way through these words. Thanks for reading *Home Sweet Texas*!

May the Lord bless you and keep you,

Sharon Gillenwater

QUESTIONS FOR DISCUSSION

1. While lost on the ranch, Sunni was determined to do everything she could to survive, including following the stream in hopes of finding help. Was that a wise thing to do? Or should she have stayed put and waited for someone to find her? What would you have done?
2. Though Sunni had no other personal memories, she was certain that God loved her and was taking care of her. Do you think God could/would reveal His love to her even under those circumstances? How can we have the reassurance of His love and faithfulness?
3. When Jake found Sunni, he considered turning her over to the sheriff and letting Toby deal with her. Why do you think he changed his mind?
4. Years earlier, Jake had slowly drifted away from the Lord. How can you stay firm in your faith and not let the world interfere

in your relationship with Jesus?

5. Jake blamed himself for Pam's death. As the much stronger Christian, he also believed he was mainly at fault because they "weren't living right" when she died. Due to his guilt and shame, he felt unworthy to seek God's grace, mercy and forgiveness. Do you have to be "worthy" to receive God's forgiveness? Do you feel guilt or shame over something that is keeping you from God's grace and mercy? Why or why not?

6. Occasionally, Sunni almost wished that her memory wouldn't return. She was happy in her new life and her growing relationship with Jake. Do you ever wish you could "wipe the slate clean" and start over with your life and relationships?

7. The folks at Kincaid Community Church came up with some creative contributions for the church auction to raise funds for the missionary trip. Does your church support missions? How does your church raise money for missions projects?

8. Sunni had tried to bury her grief and to run away from the pain, but it almost destroyed her. What are some good ways to deal with grief?

9. Licorice was one of the ring bearers in the wedding, which probably made a few

people smile. What is the most amusing thing you've seen at a wedding?

10. For most Texans, no matter where life takes them, Texas is always home, and there is no place sweeter or dearer to their hearts. Do you feel that way about your hometown? What makes it so special to you? Could you live elsewhere? Why or why not?

ABOUT THE AUTHOR

Sharon Gillenwater lives with her husband, Gene, on Washington State's beautiful Olympic Peninsula. A native of West Texas — which she sometimes desperately misses — she loves the view of the rugged Olympic Mountains from their home. The quiet, rural neighborhood is a perfect writer's retreat. Their son, Justin, and his wife, Erin, recently had their first baby, so now Sharon divides her time between writing and playing grandma to her adorable new grandson.